You're invited to a

CREEPOVER ™

Best Friends Forever

written by P. J. Night

SIMON SPOTLIGHT

New York   London   Toronto   Sydney   New Delhi

SIMON SPOTLIGHT
An imprint of Simon & Schuster Children's Publishing Division
1230 Avenue of the Americas, New York, New York 10020
Copyright © 2012 by Simon & Schuster, Inc.
All rights reserved, including the right of reproduction in whole or in part in any form.
SIMON SPOTLIGHT and colophon are registered trademarks of Simon & Schuster, Inc.
YOU'RE INVITED TO A CREEPOVER is a trademark of Simon & Schuster, Inc.
Text by Kama Einhorn
For information about special discounts for bulk purchases, please contact Simon & Schuster Special Sales at 1-866-506-1949 or business@simonandschuster.com.
Manufactured in the United States of America 0112 OFF
First Edition 10 9 8 7 6 5 4 3 2 1
ISBN 978-1-4424-4150-7
ISBN 978-1-4424-4151-4 (eBook)
This book has been cataloged with the Library of Congress

PROLOGUE

It was very early on Saturday morning, and while most other kids were sleeping, Whitney Van Lowe was wide awake and very busy.

She was unpacking her dolls, which were each in individual plastic boxes inside a larger cardboard box. Each time she opened one, it was like a reunion with an old friend. She felt a special responsibility to make the dolls comfortable in her new home.

"Penelope! I know you don't like being in your box for so long. But see, here you are in the fresh air again. Look, here's your new spot. Right next to your good friend Irene," Whitney spoke soothingly to a doll wearing a sailor suit. "You're all so lucky you don't have to go to school. I know you must hate moving around,

1

but imagine what it's like being me. I'm *always* the new girl, and I have to work so hard to make new friends."

Whitney looked at one doll in a Mexican embroidered dress. "What, Rosa?" she asked. "Yes, well, it's not as easy as it looks." She paused as if the doll was responding, and then she replied. "*Gracias.* I think you're a really good friend too!" She sighed. "I'll be back, everyone. I've got to go downstairs for breakfast."

She paused at the door, looking down at all her dolls lined up on the floor. "The name of our new town is Westbrook, everyone, remember?" she spoke like a teacher addressing a class. "It's in Connecticut. The town of Westbrook is on the beach. The body of water is Long Island Sound, and our new house is in the woods. This region of the United States is called New England. Why do you think it's called New England?" She paused.

"That's right, because English settlers moved here and started colonies." She smiled lovingly at her dolls. "Okay, there's obviously something more important that I haven't said." She sounded serious.

"I know I had to pack you in your boxes really fast. It must have been very shocking and scary. And I do know I wasn't very gentle. I'm very sorry about that. But you know that's not the way I would have done it if it had been up to me."

She took a deep breath, and her face clouded over. "I think you know that it was up to my dad, and I think you also know that *he can't be trusted.*"

Then she went downstairs, which looked like Box City. There were towers of boxes everywhere. Her dad had set up his laptop on the kitchen table and was reading something, his brow furrowed. Whitney saw him, but he didn't see her. A strange look flickered across her face as she glimpsed what was on the computer screen.

"Are you reading about Wisconsin again?" Whitney asked.

Her dad quickly closed the laptop cover. He tried to smile, but his worried expression remained. Whitney nodded knowingly. "I know you're concerned about what happened in Wisconsin," she said. "But don't worry. All that's in the past now. All I'm ever going to say about that state is that they make great cheese. And speaking of cheese, what's for breakfast?"

CHAPTER 1

That same Saturday, but hours later, in a house across town, Katie Walsh carefully applied shiny white nail polish to her best friend Amy Fitzgerald's thumbnails. She blew on them until they were dry, then added a large perfect yellow dot in the center of each. Ta-da—a sunny-side-up manicure!

"Ha! Breakfast. I love it," said Amy, opening her eyes and admiring her eggy thumbs. "Now you should make my fingernails into bacon." Katie had planned on painting them beige, to be like toast, but bacon was way better. Amy was so good at themed manicures!

Katie smiled and selected exactly the right three shades of brown and beige from Amy's collection of about fifty colors, and went to work painting bacon-y stripes on Amy's fingernails.

When Katie had finished, Amy blew on the bacon to dry it as Katie thought about eating breakfast with the Fitzgeralds tomorrow morning. It would be their last breakfast together for a long time because Amy and her family were moving from Westbrook, Connecticut, to California.

"Hey, leave it on till October, okay?" Katie said. "Keep it on till you come back to visit for Harvest Fair. And whatever you paint on my nails, I'll leave that on too. Till Harvest Fair. Which, did you realize, happens to be my birthday weekend this year? Then we'll give each other brand-new manicures."

"Of course I will," Amy said, tears springing to her eyes. "I'll cover it in clear polish if it starts to chip or wear off. And wait till you see how I'm going to do your nails on your birthday. I already have your birthday manicure planned."

Katie fought back tears of her own. "I'll cover my fingertips in Band-Aids if I have to, to keep mine on till then!" She forced a laugh. They had both promised that this slumber party would be tear free until the last possible moment, when the moving van came in the morning.

Harvest Fair felt so far away. Next week she'd start seventh grade . . . without Amy. Katie had lived next door to Amy since kindergarten, and they had always been in the same class.

Now it was Amy's turn to go to work on Katie's nails. She made Katie keep her eyes closed the entire time, even when she was blowing on them between colors. Katie was dying of curiosity, and it seemed to take forever. "Give me a hint," she kept saying. But Amy was being very strict. Finally she said, "Okay, open."

On each nail was something different. Her thumbs were watermelon slices: juicy pink background with green "rind" on the white part of the nail, and itty-bitty black dots for seeds. Her index fingernails were red-and-black ladybugs. Her middle fingernails were tiny rainbows. Her ring fingernails were painted like miniature sunsets of pink, orange, purple, and red. And her pinkies were two different shades of blue, with both pearly and matte white painted unevenly on the tips, for waves. It was Amy's best manicure ever.

"It's the 'favorite summer things' manicure," Amy explained. "So you can remember them all fall, till I come back in October."

"I don't know what to say," Katie told Amy. "I love it." She blew on each finger separately, carefully, as though she were preserving it forever. "Thanks."

"How many sleepovers have we had altogether?" Amy asked suddenly. "Do you think it's more than a hundred?" Since their houses were so close, it was easy to have a sleepover every weekend. Sometimes even on school nights.

"Just in sixth grade we've had one almost every week," said Katie, doing quick math in her head. "That's fifty-two right there. So yeah, way more than a hundred."

Amy clapped her hands the way she did when she was really happy. But she didn't look happy. "That's awesome, K," she said. They'd been calling each other "K" and "A" since the beginning of sixth grade. "We should have kept track so when we got to a hundred we could've had a special one or something. I can't believe we're only going to have them a few times a year now." Her voice broke.

"But we'll have a *really* good one for my birthday," Katie said quickly and a little more forcefully than she meant to. She supposed she was just determined not to cry. She grabbed a bottle of beige nail polish. "Okay, take off your socks. The chef is now ready to make your toes into waffles."

Katie didn't sleep well, though Amy seemed to. Amy had a trundle bed that her parents had bought just so she could have sleepovers with Katie. The bottom part of the bed pulled out to reveal a mattress that Katie slept on. It felt so good to have her own bed there—she never even needed to bring a sleeping bag like a regular slumber party.

They were both only children, and Katie thought that this might be what it was like to have a sister. Amy's parents always tucked them both in, and Katie's parents did the same when Amy slept over, though the sleepovers happened more frequently at Amy's because of the excellent trundle bed.

Amy's mom came in to wake them up early so they could all sit down to breakfast before the movers came. At first Katie forgot where she was. Then she felt happy to see Amy next to her, slowly wiggling herself awake. Then all at once she remembered the terrible truth: It was moving day. It was actually going to happen.

Today. This morning, in fact.

Amy's dad brought in breakfast from the Westbrook Diner. It was a sampling of their favorites: bacon and eggs, waffles, and banana-blueberry pancakes. Everyone ate a little of everything, and they ate off paper plates and used plastic utensils because all the kitchen stuff was already packed up.

Not that that was so new. Over the past several weeks Katie had been watching the inside of Amy's house slowly disappear. All the things she'd known and loved for so long were gone now. The wooden clock shaped like an apple with a second hand that had a bumblebee at the tip. The row of ferns on the kitchen windowsill. The big bowl of pine cones on the coffee table, picked by Amy's mom from the woods in the backyard. The framed crayon-and-watercolor picture of an owl that Amy had made in third grade when their class was studying owls. (Katie had made one too, and it was displayed in her own kitchen.) Katie had been getting sad every time she walked in the house and something new was packed up. It was as though something big and permanent in the town, like the fire station or the post office, had suddenly been torn down.

Soon the movers were carrying boxes and Amy and Katie were sitting on the back steps so they didn't have to watch.

Katie heard one of the movers talking to Amy's dad. "California, huh?" he said. "Can't get much farther from Connecticut than that, I guess!" The mover laughed as if it were the funniest thing ever.

Katie covered her face with her hands and began crying.

Amy put her arm around Katie's shoulders. "It doesn't matter how far away we are," she whispered. Katie could hear that Amy was crying too. "We're best friends. We're best friends forever."

Katie nodded, her head still in her hands. "I know," she tried to say. But she couldn't get the words out.

CHAPTER 2

Zappers is such a nice cat, Katie thought as she looked at him sideways. Her head was on her pillow and she'd been crying for while, the kind of crying where you can barely catch your breath between sobs. When she opened her eyes, there he was, purring next to her, calmly and methodically grooming himself. He always seemed to know when she was upset, and right now he provided the only company she really wanted after having come home.

Her parents had rushed over to her with sympathetic looks when she'd come in after the terrible good-bye, her dad extending his arms for a hug. She knew it was rude, but she'd ignored them both and stomped off to her bedroom, where she curled up in a ball, only getting up to let Zappers in. He had been meowing and pawing at her locked door.

Zappers was a big, long-haired black cat who Katie and her parents had adopted from the local shelter a few years ago. Looking at him now, it seemed he'd always lived here. Katie remembered how when they first brought him home, her parents had joked that she finally had a sibling—a "fur brother," they called him. It seemed so funny at the time—*a fur brother!*—but thinking of it now only made Katie cry harder. *Amy was like my sister,* she thought over and over.

She remembered how she and Amy had once even lied to Santa about being sisters. *Lied to Santa!* They were in third grade, and their dads had taken them to the mall to see Santa. They waited in line together and insisted on sitting on Santa's lap together so they could be in the same picture.

"Ho, ho, ho, what have we here?" Santa said kindly. "Are you girls sisters?"

Just as Katie was about to say "No, but we're best friends," Amy said, "Yes, Santa, we are."

She said it with a straight face. Katie nodded happily in agreement, not daring to make eye contact with Amy because she knew she would start laughing uncontrollably. Since then, just saying the phrase "Yes, Santa, we are" was enough to make them both crack up. And sometimes, out of the blue, one of them would say to the other, "Remember when we lied to Santa?"

Living next door to each other, they'd gone in and out of each other's homes without even knocking. Their parents even had keys to each other's houses, for when they went on vacation and needed to feed the cat or water the plants or check that the heat was still on. One time Amy's family was away and there was a blizzard, and Katie and her mom shoveled the Fitzgeralds' sidewalk and driveway so the mail could be delivered and the Fitzgeralds could park their car when they got home. It was such hard work that once they got up to the door, Katie's mom unlocked it, and they both took off their coats and boots, collapsed on the couch for a while, and watched television before checking on the rest of the house. Katie had sent Amy a text message that read U O ME BIG-TIME!

Katie had never before felt lonely being an only child. Now suddenly she felt a wave of loneliness wash over her. Actually, it felt more like it was knocking her down in the sand, so hard she could barely breathe. That had happened to her at the beach once.

Zappers was now staring at her intently with his green-gold eyes, looking sort of startled.

"Oh, Zappers," Katie whispered, stroking his fur. "Don't look so puzzled. It's called crying. Humans do it, remember? It's like meowing." This did not seem to help him understand.

She got up—her whole body felt so heavy—and went to the bathroom to get a tissue. She felt kind of dazed and dizzy. Then she heard her parents calling up to her.

"Kookaburra, come downstairs soon," her dad was saying. He'd given her that nickname when she was born; Katie wasn't sure why. But it had stuck. They both called her that a lot, sometimes just "Kooka."

"I'll be down in a minute," Katie called. She examined her red, puffy eyes in the mirror. Her head hurt from crying so hard, and she was suddenly very thirsty. *I guess crying is hard work,* she thought. She splashed her face with cold water and blew her nose again, then started down the stairs.

"Oh, Kooka," her mom said when she saw her. She turned off the television. "Come sit with us." Her mom moved over on the couch so Katie could sit between her parents. Katie suddenly felt like a little girl, not someone about to start seventh grade. She sat in her designated spot and felt a little bit like she was in a nest.

She had to admit it felt good. Her mom was a child psychologist, and at moments like these Katie understood what made her so good at her job. Katie knew her mom wasn't going to tell her not to be sad or try to distract her, like another parent might do. She was just inviting Katie to be sad on the couch with them. That was good because there was absolutely no way Katie was not going to be sad.

Katie's dad put his arm around her. "I'm really going to miss the Fitzgeralds too," he said. "They were such great neighbors. They felt like family, right?" he said to Katie's mom.

Katie's mom nodded slowly. "I remember when Jeanette and Jerry and Amy moved in," she told Katie. "You and Amy were both such little dumplings! Wow, you had barely started preschool. We were so happy that a little girl your age had moved into that house. And look at what wound up happening. You two became best friends almost right away."

This made Katie start to cry again. "Moving doesn't change the fact that you're best friends, honey," Katie's mom said. "Once someone's in your heart the way Amy is, they're there for good. Things will be different. It's going to take time to get used to not having her right there. But you're going to be okay."

Her dad nodded in agreement. "It must be hard to think about starting school next week without Amy," he added. "It's sad for me to start classes without Jerry on campus too." Katie's dad was a psychology professor, and Amy's dad was a history professor. They had both taught at Wesleyan University, which was about a half hour away, and sometimes drove together. But Amy's dad had gotten a new job at some college in California. *Some stupid college in California,* Katie thought, suddenly furious with Mr. Fitzgerald.

"Poor Amy, having to start in a totally new school without knowing anyone at all," Katie said. "I wish I could go with her to her first day of school."

"Yes. She's going to have to work at making some new friends, just like you are," her mom said. "You're both going to have to be brave, that first day."

But Katie wasn't really listening because her phone,

which was in her shorts pocket, had started to vibrate. Yay—a text from Amy!

HEY K——I LOVE MY BACON & EGGS. MISS U
SO MUCH CANT WAIT 2 C U IN 6 WKS! WE R
GETTING ON PLANE NOW, UP, UP & AWAY ☹
☹ ☹——BFF

Katie shot back:

A, WAVE DOWN TO ME WHEN YOU TAKE OFF.
I JUST CRIED ALL OVER ZAPPERS! I MISS U SO
MUCH ALREADY!——BFF

Almost immediately, Amy replied:

"YES, SANTA, WE ARE."——BFF

Katie didn't know you could laugh and cry at the same time, but that's what she did.

CHAPTER 3

School started on a Wednesday. The fact that it was already midway through the week made it a little easier to face. The other thing that made it somewhat bearable was the fact that Amy would be back for Katie's birthday in six weeks. Washing her hands and face the morning of the first day, Katie was pleasantly distracted by her fingernails. Having Amy's miniature masterpieces on her hands seemed to give Katie a secret power, the courage to make it through the day.

Sometimes she would stare at one nail until she got lost in it and its matching memory. For example, the waves and water on her pinky finger looked so much like a three-dimensional wave. Katie would remember days at the beach with Amy, playing in the waves, staying there all day, till the late afternoon summer sun started getting lower in the sky.

Or she would look at the ladybugs, which for some reason were the only bugs she and Amy ever found in their houses that summer. "I guess if we're going to be infested, it's nice that it's with ladybugs," her mom had joked with Amy's dad. "Katie loves them; she wouldn't dream of us spraying to get rid of them."

Katie had been careful over the last week to keep her manicure perfect, and she didn't have one chip. Amy had told her last night over the phone that the same was true for her.

Katie had heard how different seventh grade was from sixth grade. It was in a different building from sixth grade. But the main difference, besides Amy not being there, seemed to be that the kids had lockers and a schedule that had them hopping from class to class all day. There was also homeroom, which met for about fifteen minutes first thing in the morning. Katie was assigned to Mr. Armstrong's homeroom, along with ten other kids. Mr. Armstrong was young and funny and seemed to really like his job. He asked them to move their chairs into a circle. There was a new girl, who he introduced.

"Welcome to seventh grade, everyone," he said. "This year we have a newcomer to Westbrook and to our school, so let's introduce ourselves to her. Everyone, this is Whitney Van Lowe, and she's just moved here from Wisconsin. Okay, let's go around the circle. Everyone say your name and one fun thing you did this summer."

This summer I said good-bye to my best friend, and it wasn't fun at all, Katie thought, but by the time it was her turn she'd thought of something normal to say.

"I went on a hot-air balloon ride with Amy on her birthday," she said.

"Wow," Mr. Armstrong said. "Has anyone else ever been in a hot-air balloon?" No one had.

"And who's Amy?" Mr. Armstrong said.

Katie took a deep breath. "She's my best friend," she said. "She just moved. To California."

"I see," said Mr. Armstrong. "Okay, Ben, your turn."

"I went on a canoe trip at camp," Ben said. "And I ate a raw hot dog and didn't get sick." Everyone laughed.

"Congratulations, Ben," said Mr. Armstrong. "Whitney?"

It was Whitney's turn. She kept her head down, looking at her lap, but didn't say anything. There was an uncomfortable silence, during which Katie thought that Whitney must be very shy or supernervous to speak. But Whitney just didn't seem to realize it was her turn. At last Mr. Armstrong said, "And how about you, Whitney? What was one fun thing you did this summer? Besides move to Westbrook, of course." He laughed at his own joke.

Once Whitney finally looked up, Katie realized how pretty the new girl was. She had very pale skin, black hair cut really short, in what Katie knew was called a "pixie cut" because her aunt Lindsay had the same haircut, and very light blue eyes.

"I got a new doll," Whitney said quietly.

Mr. Armstrong paused. He smiled and nodded in a way that let the group know not to snicker. Katie figured most of the girls in seventh grade would say they were too old for dolls. If they did still have dolls, they certainly wouldn't announce that getting a doll was a fun thing they did over the summer. Then Mr. Armstrong said, "Great. Okay, Brendan, your turn." And on it went.

Rachel and Emma were also in the homeroom, and they had barely looked up as Whitney was talking. Katie and Amy had hung out with Rachel and Emma in fifth and sixth grade, even having a few sleepovers. Rachel and Emma were best friends too. But they had barely spoken to her this morning. Rachel seemed to be pouting about something, and Emma was preoccupied with her notebook.

"Hey, you guys!" Katie had said when they entered the room. They both smiled, and Rachel said, "Hey. Have you heard from Amy? She hasn't returned my e-mail." She sounded annoyed.

"Um, yeah," Katie said, not sure how to respond. "She's doing okay. They're in their new place, but the movers still haven't come, so she's sleeping on a blow-up mattress and living out of her suitcase!" Katie thought that was an interesting detail to share with them, but Emma rolled her eyes. *What's up with that?* Katie thought.

She spent her free period writing a letter to Amy.

A, hey! Hey, A! Ha-ha. It's not even lunchtime and the first day is feeling loooong. I bet you are on your way to your first day now. I can never remember what the time difference is, but I think it is three hours earlier where you are, right? I hope your day goes okay. I miss you so much, it is SO WEIRD here without you. Rachel and Emma are being kind of cold, too. You know what I was thinking about Harvest Fair? I was thinking that this year should be the year we go into the fun house (or haunted house, whatever it is called). I don't think it's that scary, I mean I heard it's not that scary. What do you think? We are in seventh grade, after all, and how bad can it be if we do it together? I promise not to dig my fingernails into your arm like I did when we got so freaked out last Halloween. Speaking of which, you know what? My fingernails are still perfect, and I think the watermelon is my favorite. I miss, miss, miss, miss, miss you. I wrote it five times so you know I mean it. Oh well, it is time for lunch. Where am I going to sit? You are probably eating breakfast now. Don't eat your fingernails! Get it? Or your waffle toes, either. Ick.

Love, K (BFF)

The time Katie had spent writing the letter was the most "herself" she had felt all day. It was as if the rest of the day, she was onstage in a play, and writing to Amy, she was backstage relaxing.

Before lunch, though, the day took a turn for the worse. Everyone had assigned lockers, and Mr. Armstrong had given out the combinations and demonstrated how to work the locks. Katie's combination was 16, 7, 9. You turned a little dial three times, switching direction each time, and the locker would open. Great, except that it just didn't work. Katie tried again and again, each time feeling more and more flustered. She looked up to see Whitney staring at her.

"I'm really good at these," Whitney told her. She spoke softly and evenly. "Do you want me to try?"

Now Katie was even more embarrassed. The new girl was offering to help—wasn't it supposed to be the new girl who had locker trouble? But her gratitude soon outweighed her embarrassment, and Katie stepped aside.

"Yes, please! Sixteen, seven, nine!" She smiled, trying to seem cool about it. She let Whitney go to work, not even thinking she should watch and learn for next time.

Then Katie saw it. She'd chipped her index fingernail

on the lock. The ladybug's head was gone.

"What's the matter?" Whitney asked, seeming not quite as shy as before.

"Oh, it's okay. I just broke my nail," Katie said. Suddenly her nails felt very private, but Whitney was moving in for a look.

"Oh, how pretty," Whitney exclaimed, looking carefully at each one. "Sorry about your ladybug."

"Thanks," Katie said. "Well, thanks for helping me. And welcome to our school." She gave a little wave and started walking away, but Whitney said, "Can you show me to the cafeteria?" She seemed shy and nervous again.

"Sure," Katie said. It seemed like the right thing to do. They walked together in silence, and Katie realized that Whitney might want to sit down and eat with her. At first she felt anxious about this, but then she realized that she didn't want to sit with Rachel and Emma the way she'd assumed she would. And she wasn't sure they wanted to sit with her, either, though she had no idea why.

Whitney must be anxious too, Katie thought. *Just like Amy is today. Just like me.*

"Why don't you sit with me?" Katie heard herself ask. Whitney broke into a grin and nodded gratefully. As they sat and ate, Katie was surprised by how comfortable she felt. Whitney was actually pretty chatty. She asked Katie lots of questions about herself and her family, and listened carefully to the answers. Had she lived here her whole life? Did she get good grades? What did her parents do? How long had she and Amy lived next door to each other? How was she doing since Amy had moved away?

"I move a lot," Whitney said. "So I understand how hard it is. I get used to being the new kid, but since it's Amy's first time, it can't be easy."

Katie felt touched by Whitney's sensitivity. She knew she should say something nice in return.

"But you must get pretty tired of being new."

"Yeah," said Whitney. "But I learn to make friends. And now I have friends from all over the world. Hey, I know we just met, but why don't you come over on Saturday? My room is finally set up. You could even sleep over!"

A sleepover with a total stranger? That's a little fast, no? Katie thought. But she heard her mom's voice in her head saying she would have to push herself a little to make new friends. And she knew it was true. Well, maybe it would happen more easily than she'd thought. Here was Whitney, who seemed really nice. Before she lost her nerve or thought better of it, she made up her mind. "Okay," she said before she could stop herself. "I'll ask my parents. Saturday is usually movie night, but it's probably fine."

"Movie night," Whitney said slowly, as if she had never heard of such a thing. Then suddenly she asked, "Are you an only child?"

"Yeah," Katie said. "How'd you know? Well, my parents *are* really into having movie night with me. What about you? Are you an only child?" Katie had a feeling that she was, though she couldn't explain why.

"Yes, Katie, I am," Whitney said. It reminded Katie of Amy's superserious delivery of the line, "Yes, Santa, we are," and it made her smile inside. Seventh grade might not be a total disaster after all. Of course, it wouldn't be great. But so far, it wasn't a nightmare.

That night, Katie's parents took her out for pizza to Sal's, a new restaurant in town. As soon as they were seated, her pocket vibrated.

K, THE FIRST DAY WAS REALLY GOOD, ACTUALLY!
I LOVE MY HOMEROOM.——BFF

Right, it was about seven o'clock here, so it was four o'clock in the afternoon in California. Katie wrote back:

A, WOW, THAT'S REALLY GREAT. MINE WAS OKAY. NOT BAD, NOT GREAT.——BFF

Amy wrote right back:

K, OH NO! I'LL CALL YOU LATER. MY STUDY BUDDY KIRA IS HERE.——BFF

Katie wrote:

WHAT'S A STUDY BUDDY?——BFF

It took Amy about a half hour to respond. Katie distracted herself by eating pizza. The pizzeria had crayons to use on the white paper tablecloth, and when she was finished eating, she doodled while her parents talked. Finally she felt a vibration.

SHE'S IN MY HOMEROOM. EVERYONE GOT PAIRED
UP WITH A STUDY BUDDY, AND WE ARE SUPPOSED
TO HELP EACH OTHER ALL YEAR. LIKE IF WE HAVE
QUESTIONS ABOUT HOMEWORK OR WHATEVER.
SHE LIVES A FEW HOUSES AWAY, SO SHE CAME
OVER AFTER SCHOOL TO HELP ME ORGANIZE. YOU
KNOW HOW MUCH I NEED IT. HA-HA.——BFF

"Did you get much homework?" Katie's mom asked as she took another slice of pizza. "Wow, I really like this place. I was worried when Zino's closed, but I think this is even better."

"They didn't give much homework the first day of school, but I have to set up my binder a certain way, and I don't remember how," Katie mumbled. She went back to her doodle.

"Can you call someone for help?" her dad asked.

"Well, I don't have my very own *study buddy*," Katie said sarcastically. She didn't realize how bitter she felt about Amy mentioning this Kira until she heard the tone of her own voice.

Her dad looked at her, puzzled. Katie explained the text exchanges with Amy.

"I see. Sounds like Amy had a better first day than you. Well, study buddies actually seem like a pretty good idea for seventh grade. Everyone could use one of those," he said.

"I guess," Katie said. "Anyway, you'll both be very pleased. There's a new girl, and I think we're going to be friends." She noticed a look of relief on her parents' faces.

"Her name is Whitney, and she's pretty nice. I sat with her at lunch," Katie continued. Her mom seemed to be trying to keep herself from applauding. "Try to control yourself, Mom," Katie said teasingly.

"I'm sorry, Kookaburra." Her mother smiled. "The first day can be hard, and making new friends can be scary. I'm so proud of you."

"Where did Whitney move here from?" her dad asked as he reached over and grabbed her mom's crust off her plate.

"Um, Wisconsin," said Katie. "And guess what? She invited me for a sleepover on Saturday. I said I'd ask, but now I think it's too soon. Maybe I'll just tell her you said no."

"Oh, Kooka," her dad said. "I think you should

30

push yourself a little. You're a good judge of character, and all we were going to do Saturday night was watch a movie. We could just do it Sunday instead. Go have a sleepover with your new friend. You've been in the house all week."

CHAPTER 4

Thursday and Friday at school went fine. Katie ate lunch with Whitney both days. They had only Spanish and homeroom together, so they just saw each other then and at lunch. Katie could open her locker easily now and hung out a little with Emma and Rachel, who were in some of her classes, though somehow it didn't feel very natural. Actually, what it felt like was "three's a crowd." But Saturday came pretty fast.

Katie's dad whistled as they drove along the winding roads that led to Whitney's house. The whistling was kind of annoying, a rather tuneless tune, but Katie didn't want to hurt her dad's feelings. She had noticed her parents being extra nice to her since Amy had moved away.

"Hey, Kookaburra," her dad said. "How about us having build-your-own taco bar tomorrow night before the movie? Sunday night special."

"Yeah, definitely," Katie said. "With superspicy salsa."

"You got it," her dad said. "And lots and lots of olives," he added teasingly. He knew olives tasted like poison to Katie. She groaned but was secretly pleased about the plans for the taco bar. Her parents had been making her favorite dinners and patiently sitting with her through television shows she knew they didn't like. Their attempts to cheer her up weren't that helpful, but it was sweet they cared.

Whitney's family lived across town, in a neighborhood Katie had never been to. "You'd think I know every street in town by now," she said. After all, she'd lived here her whole life and had spent plenty of time in the car with her parents.

"Believe it or not, I've never been to this neighborhood either," her dad told her. "Keep looking for Alabaster Way, okay? I can hardly see with this glare."

Katie squinted in the afternoon sun for another mile, anxious they had already missed the turn. How much longer should they go before turning around and backtracking? "There it is!" she crowed triumphantly as she pointed to the street sign. Her dad made a left turn, and they both craned their necks to see the house numbers until they found the small brick home Whitney had described. When they finally pulled into the driveway, Katie was surprised at the nervous feeling in her stomach. It was the same way she felt before a dance recital.

"You have your phone, right?" her dad asked, smiling at her reassuringly.

"Yup," she answered, trying for a casual tone. How did he know how uneasy she suddenly felt? It *did* always make her feel better to have her cell phone with her, knowing she could call her parents anywhere, anytime. *What's up with me?* she thought. *I've been on at least a hundred sleepovers.*

"Okay then," her dad said. "Call us to say hello, if you like."

Katie grabbed her stuff—a purple sleeping bag with a built-in pillow and matching overnight bag—and walked up to the door with her dad, hoping she didn't look as nervous as she felt. Whitney was already standing in the open doorway.

"Hi!" Whitney exclaimed in a voice that seemed a little too loud. She looked relieved that Katie had arrived. "Was it hard to find my house? Were my directions okay?"

"Hey, Whitney," Katie said shyly. "No, the directions were fine." She noticed that Whitney's eyes seemed even lighter and bluer than they had in school, if that was even possible. As she and her dad stepped inside, Katie felt a bit better as she realized that Whitney was just as nervous as she was. She thought back to that morning at breakfast, when her mom had caught her eye and said, "Listen, honey, I know it's hard trying to make new friends."

"Whatever," Katie had mumbled, staring into her cereal. She hadn't meant for her response to sound as rude as it did.

But her mom had continued in the same kind tone. "Well, I think you and Whitney are brave to push forward and have a sleepover, even though you don't know each other very well yet."

"Thanks," Katie said as her eyes welled up. Luckily, she stopped herself from crying before her tears started dripping into her bowl, which would've made her sweet cereal taste salty.

Okay, maybe Mom was right, she thought now. *Maybe this sleepover's going to be worth it.*

Katie's dad walked her up the door, and when she went to kiss him good-bye, she realized he would want to meet Whitney's parents. "Um, are your parents around?" she asked Whitney.

"It's just my dad. Dad!" Whitney called, not taking her eyes off Katie or her dad. Soon Whitney's dad came into the hallway. He reached out to shake Katie's dad's hand.

"Clay Van Lowe," he said. Katie's dad smiled and shook Mr. Van Lowe's hand.

"Bernard Walsh," Katie's dad said. "Welcome to Westbrook. And thanks for having Katie tonight."

Katie felt giggly. Dads introduced themselves in a funny way. She imagined shaking hands with Amy and saying in deep voices, "Katie Walsh" and "Amy Fitzgerald."

"Okay, then, Kooka," her dad said a few moments later. "See you tomorrow. I'll pick you up at noon."

"Bye, Dad," Katie said. She gave him a quick hug and found herself wanting to keep hugging him, but made herself stop. Then he waved good-bye to everyone and left.

Judging by the way Whitney's living room looked, there wasn't a whole lot of living going on there, just open boxes, piles of books, an unplugged television on the floor, and a couch standing on its side. Katie noticed a worried look on Whitney's face.

"My room is all fixed up," Whitney said quickly, sliding between Katie and the rest of the living room. "Come on. I'll show you."

Katie turned to follow Whitney upstairs. Whitney opened the door to her room with a flourish.

"Ta-da!" she sang proudly. Katie took in the room: a pale pink frilly bed with a few lacy throw pillows, a little wooden desk with nothing on it at all, and a small framed oil painting of a unicorn drinking from a pond turned silver by moonlight.

"Pretty room," Katie said diplomatically.

"Thanks. I decorated it myself."

Whitney looked at her expectantly, and Katie tried to think of something else to say. "I used to collect unicorns," she offered.

The sentence hung awkwardly in the air as another wave of sadness washed over Katie. How she wished she would be sleeping in Amy's trundle bed tonight instead of on the floor in her sleeping bag in this strange room.

Amy's walls had been covered with some of the same movie and music posters Katie had in her room at home, pulled carefully out of the same magazines. There was also a desk with a computer where they would spend hours playing games. Sometimes Amy's mom would bring in a giant bowl of her famous peanut-butter popcorn and the girls would be so happy they'd jump up and give her a standing ovation. There were also two big beanbags perfect for eating popcorn in.

By comparison, Whitney's room looked like a room Katie's grandmother might have lived in as a little girl.

Then Katie noticed she had an audience.

All around the room, on the bed and on the floor, sat about twenty porcelain dolls. Each doll was a little different—different dresses and hair colors—but they all were sitting up straight and wearing fancy clothes that made them seem old-fashioned.

"Wow, that's a lot of dolls," Katie said.

"Twenty, to be exact." Whitney beamed. "I've been collecting them for a long time."

All these dolls seem really babyish for a seventh grader, Katie thought. But then she remembered how not so long ago, toward the end of sixth grade, she had put her favorite dolls into a box destined for the attic. She had decided that middle school girls were too old to play with dolls, which felt a little sad. To comfort herself, she vowed to keep Seymour, the stuffed monkey with the oversize head that she'd had since she was a baby. By now Katie hardly ever thought about her dolls, but she still slept with Seymour every night. And she had to admit, she had no plans to stop.

In fact, the strange porcelain dolls made her wish she had brought Seymour. Seymour was soft and fuzzy and well-worn, the opposite of these clean, stiff, perfect dolls. Holding him would make it so much easier to relax and fall asleep.

"I like unicorns," Whitney said. "But dolls are what I collect."

"Cool," Katie replied, not knowing what else to say.

"I know, right?" Whitney said brightly. "Anyway, you can put your stuff over there." She indicated the one doll-free corner of the room.

Katie put her overnight bag in the designated spot, but still clutched her sleeping bag. She squeezed it to her chest as hard as she could and imagined her parents at home eating Chinese take-out. It would be nice to be there with them. She and Amy had taught themselves to use chopsticks right before Amy moved away, the two of them practicing for hours on Amy's bedroom floor, using wooden take-out chopsticks and marshmallows. They quickly became pros, and Katie was eager to show off for her parents.

"Do you want to make art?" Whitney asked, pulling out a box full of art supplies. Katie had never heard that expression before, "make art." It sounded weird. Then Whitney started to draw without waiting for an answer. But when Katie saw what she was drawing with—these pens that looked like Magic Markers, but came out like glittery paint—she was immediately into it. The two lay on the floor on their stomachs and drew and talked. Katie drew fireworks. The glitter markers made them look so real.

"I love that," Whitney said, noticing Katie's drawing. "I really love that."

Katie smiled shyly. "Thanks. These are cool pens," she said as she continued making her luminous fireworks burst on the page. "You know what? There are fireworks on the beach here on the Fourth of July. It's fun."

Whitney seemed enthusiastic about the possibility of fireworks on the beach. "I've never lived this close to the beach," she said.

"I think you'll like it," Katie said. "This summer there were more hermit crabs in the water than ever before," she added. She thought, *It's going to be fine. Whitney's nice. She just hasn't put her dolls away yet.*

Whitney stared at Katie and smiled widely. "Let's play dolls now," she said.

Katie couldn't believe that Whitney was actually suggesting that they play dolls, but she reminded herself that moving to a new town was probably even lonelier than having your best friend move away. Whitney probably liked having company, even if it was pretend company. She took a deep breath to relax herself. But all she got was a noseful of mothball smell.

CHAPTER 5

Whitney didn't seem to notice Katie's apprehension. She'd already sat down against the wall like one of the dolls and crisscrossed her legs.

"Crisscross applesauce!" Whitney said happily to Katie as she patted her own thighs, indicating that Katie should sit in the same position. Katie couldn't help but remember that her kindergarten teacher used to say the same thing at circle time.

Whitney picked up a doll with shiny black hair in ringlet curls. "Now *you* choose a friend," she instructed Katie, gesturing to the rows of dolls as if she were inviting Katie to do the most normal thing in the world.

Katie remembered how she used to think her dolls were really her friends. *But dolls aren't my friends,* she thought now. *Amy was my friend. My real friend.* She smiled weakly and looked around at all the dolls as if she were really choosing one, so Whitney wouldn't know how silly and strange she thought this whole doll thing was.

"Okay, thanks. I will," Katie said, carefully keeping the judgmental tone out of her voice.

She picked up a doll with ash-colored blond braids and bangs. This unfortunate doll wore a sailor suit with anchors embroidered on it. Holding the doll, Katie sat down on the floor across from Whitney. *I can't believe we're playing with dollies like two little girls,* she thought. *I hope Whitney doesn't want to have a tea party. I wonder how long before dinner. I wonder what we're having.*

Whitney had another wide, odd grin on her face. She seemed thrilled that Katie had chosen a doll.

"That's Penelope," she told Katie as if she were a mother introducing her toddler to another child. "She's new!" Katie guessed that this must be the doll Whitney had mentioned in homeroom, the new doll she got this summer. *I guess it's sweet that Whitney's such an attentive doll mom,* Katie thought. *She's named each one and obviously takes good care of them. Maybe that means she'll be a good friend.*

Katie politely examined Penelope, trying to show appreciation for the doll's beauty.

"Penelope's a sailor, " Whitney explained. "And she's really good at checkers."

"She's pretty," Katie said. And it was true, the doll was pretty. She even had dimples. She also had the kind of doll eyes that open and close, and Katie fingered one of the eyelids so it would look like she was winking. The eyelid was lined with shiny plastic black lashes, stiff as the bristles on a toothbrush.

"Well, say hello to her," Whitney told Katie. She sounded slightly impatient.

Katie couldn't believe what she was hearing, but she played along without missing a beat. She looked at Penelope's face and made eye contact with her as if she were a real person. "Hi, Penelope. How are you? You have such pretty eyes."

Then she noticed that the doll's eyeballs didn't look as fake as most dolls' eyes.

They were plastic, but somehow . . . different. They made Katie think of a dog food commercial she had seen in which real dogs were smiling with human lips and teeth. But that commercial was made with special effects from a computer, and this was real life.

"Penelope is from Wisconsin, but her family heritage is Dutch!" Whitney said with obvious pride. "I lived in Amsterdam for a little while a few years ago, so I know all about the Dutch."

"Oh, really?" Katie looked closer at the eyes. It seemed like Penelope's irises were the same pale, bright blue as Whitney's. They were as light as blue could get without being called white. The black pupils looked like they went deep into her eyes, like they were letting in light, and the whites of her eyes were shiny and moist, like a person's. Katie could even see faint red squiggles in them—veins.

And then Penelope's eyes looked right at Katie. Right into her eyes.

The nervous feeling Katie had felt in her stomach in Whitney's driveway now moved through her whole body.

She felt it on the soles of her feet and on her scalp. Every cell of her body froze as she looked back into Penelope's eyes, somehow unable to look away.

Penelope's face and body remained perfectly still and doll-like, but her eyes stared at Katie.

Katie started talking herself down the way she did when she was babysitting and heard the house creaking.

You've just had too much candy today, she said to herself, as if she was her mother talking to her. *Too much sugar makes you a little cuckoo, remember, Kookaburra?*

She tried to focus on something else. Whitney was now combing another doll's hair with a tiny comb. Katie tried to listen to her quick, cheerful chatter.

"My dolls *really* don't like to get packed up in boxes and go into the moving van," Whitney was saying. "So here's what I do. I feed them candy first. Veronica here likes lemon drops, but this one, Irene? She only eats lollipops. And Rosa is from Mexico. Do you know what she likes? Candied rose petals. Seriously."

What on earth was she talking about?

Whitney continued, "Oh, Irene, *no.*" She sighed. "You already had your lollipop today."

Focus, focus, Katie told herself. Whitney was still yapping away. "And some of them will wear only velvet and others insist on satin. . . ."

Katie was still locked into Penelope's eyes and just trying to keep breathing—it felt like all the air had been sucked out of her lungs by a vacuum—when she felt herself being watched.

Watched not just by Penelope, but by every doll in the room.

Forty eyes were all staring directly, silently, insistently, at her.

CHAPTER 6

A figment of your imagination, a figment of your imagination, Katie said over and over to herself as if it were a spell that could erase what she had just experienced. This had to be something she was imagining.

"It's great to have such a good imagination, Kooka," her mom would say gently when Katie was little and telling fibs. "But maybe sometimes you get a little confused between what's real and what's pretend?"

Remembering this made Katie feel better. Then she remembered how she and Amy used to scare themselves during sleepovers, telling ghost stories or imagining noises in the house in the middle of the night. Everything was always okay in the end. There was never any ghost or burglar. In the morning, it all seemed so silly. Katie's heartbeat was starting to slow down, and she could breathe normally again.

Just as Katie realized she was getting pretty hungry, Whitney's dad appeared at the door with a big tray of food.

Katie was thrilled. One, that she didn't have to sit down at a table with him and Whitney, because sometimes she got shy in front of other people's parents. And two, it was such a treat to eat in Whitney's room off a tray. Katie only got to eat in her room off a tray when she was sick.

"Thank you," Katie said to Whitney's dad. Whitney said nothing. She actually didn't even look up and acknowledge that her dad had come in.

"You're welcome," Whitney's dad said.

"Do you girls have everything you need?" he asked, reminding Katie of a waiter.

Whitney looked carefully at the tray. "Is this bagel plain or whole wheat? It looks like whole wheat," she said.

"It's plain. The kind you like. They're from a different bakery, so they look a little different," her dad said, sounding nervous. "But it's plain."

"Oh," Whitney said. "Then yes, we have everything we need."

"Great," her dad said, and closed the door. But then he opened it again. Whitney seemed really annoyed.

"I was going to hang your shelves in the morning," her dad said. "Do you want them to go all around the room, or just on two walls? Your collection is getting so big, you may need more space."

"Oh, I don't need shelves this time," Whitney said, not looking at her father. "My dolls have told me that they don't want to be on shelves."

"Really?" her dad said.

"As I said, no shelves this time," Whitney said flatly.

Her dad seemed surprised. "You'll have a lot of clutter if you keep them on the bed and the floor. Where will you put your—"

But Whitney interrupted. "Can you let it go?" she snapped rudely. "Actually, you know what? You're really starting to upset me. Exactly the way Mommy used to."

"I'm sorry, honey," her dad said quickly. "No shelves, then. No problem." He left quietly, closing the door softly behind him.

Katie had absorbed the tension of this exchange

between Whitney and her dad. Her shoulders were practically up to her ears. She took a deep breath.

Whitney's dad made Katie feel uneasy, though she couldn't figure out why. It was true she was shy at first around other people's parents, but she got a very strange vibe from Mr. Van Lowe. Then she realized what it was: He had not looked at her. Not at all, from the moment she walked in. *That's really strange, to not even look at a person who comes into your house,* she thought.

But it turned out to be easy to forget the weirdness, because what was before them on the tray was like a dream dinner. There was a bowl of french fries. A few mini cinnamon croissants spread with peanut butter, honey, and banana and cut into bite-size pieces. And a tuna melt on a cut-up bagel. A *plain* bagel, Katie now knew.

The tray included every single one of Whitney's favorite foods. Katie knew this because in homeroom the day before, everyone was asked to tell their favorite foods, and these were the three on Whitney's list. Each girl took a plate and napkin and dug in.

Whitney cut her french fries up with a knife and fork, which Katie thought was strange, but she didn't say anything.

For dessert, there was a bowl of grapes and a bowl of purple and green jellybeans. As Katie took a grape, she noticed it felt different from other grapes. Slimier, somehow. She looked at the grape in her hand and realized it didn't have any skin on it.

"The grapes are all peeled?" she asked Whitney incredulously.

"Oh, yeah," Whitney replied casually. "I don't like the peels, so my dad takes them off."

"Wow," said Katie. "That must take a really long time."

"Whatever," Whitney said. "Well, I'm going to get into my nightgown. I'll use the bathroom first, then you can change in there too."

Katie nodded but couldn't help thinking of the nighttime routine at Amy's. They never worried about changing into pajamas privately, first of all. That had never even occurred to them. Second of all, a nightgown? Katie had been sleeping in big T-shirts since fifth grade. For tonight, she'd packed a T-shirt and a pair of her dad's boxer shorts that she'd made her own. But there was Whitney, emerging from the bathroom in a long, frilly nightgown with flowers all over it.

Katie went into the bathroom to change, then came out and unrolled her sleeping bag next to Whitney's bed. She dug in her bag for her cell phone and placed it by her head, noticing that her mom had sent her a text message.

HOPE YOU'RE HAVING FUN, KOOKABURRA. SWEET DREAMS!

Katie quickly responded:

THANKS, IT'S GOING OKAY, I GUESS. GIVE ZAPPERS A SCRITCHY-SCRATCH FOR ME.

Whitney turned off the lights. She still slept with a night-light, and even though Katie had stopped using hers at home, she was suddenly grateful there was one here.

"Who do you have for science again?" Katie asked Whitney after both girls has settled into their beds.

"Ms. Barrish," Whitney responded. "I like her. We're going to choose our own projects."

"Cool," said Katie. "I have Mr. Keitel. I don't know

what the deal is with projects yet."

"I'm going to research the circulatory system," Whitney said. "Did you know that your heart is a muscle?"

"Really?" Katie thought for a minute. "No, I didn't know that. But we took our pulses yesterday in gym to measure our heart rate. By the way, Ms. Hall, who teaches gym, is really nice. But I'm trying to think of things you *really* need to know about living here."

"Thanks," said Whitney. "I appreciate that." Sometimes Whitney's speech really sounded like a grown-up's. *Thanks, I appreciate that.* It was something Katie could imagine her mother saying on the phone. Katie figured Whitney spent a lot of time around grown-ups, being an only child. Of course, Katie always had Amy nearby to talk to, and she would often go a whole day without talking to grown-ups.

"Okay, I thought of the most important thing," Katie said, feeling happiness rise in her chest with the memory of what she was about to share. "Every fall here on the town green there's a Harvest Fair. There are hayrides, pumpkin-carving contests, fireworks, and here's the best part. There's this booth where you can dip your own apples in caramel or chocolate, or both. Then you dip the apple in something else, like coconut or chocolate chips or crushed Oreos or sprinkles and things like that."

"I love caramel," Whitney said.

"Me too. But I highly recommend first a thin layer of caramel, then a few dips of chocolate," Katie added. "Then . . . I dip the whole thing in M&M's!"

"Oh my God!" Whitney cackled. The two of them laughed at the over-the-top craziness of the idea. Then suddenly Whitney yelled loudly, "DAD!"

Her dad appeared in the doorway almost immediately. "Yes, honey?" he asked.

"Night water," Whitney said simply.

"Be right back," her dad said, and returned with a glass of water. He handed it to her.

"For Katie, too," Whitney said.

"Sure," he said. He brought Katie one too.

"Thanks," Katie said. She didn't usually need water during the night, but Whitney seemed intent on her dad bringing her some. She was really surprised that Whitney ordered her dad around like that and didn't say please or thank you. Katie's dad would have been like,

"Sorry, Your Royal Highness. The butler has the day off." But then again . . . Katie would never have *wanted* to talk to her parents like that either.

"You're welcome," Whitney's dad said. "Good night, girls."

He still didn't look at Katie, even when he was putting the water by her on the floor.

"Good night," they said in unison. Her dad closed the door.

"Want to play a game till we fall asleep?" Whitney asked Katie.

"Sure," Katie said, feeling a little relieved at the idea. She had been slightly worried that she wouldn't be able to fall asleep easily. There was nothing worse for her than lying in bed, anxious about falling asleep, watching the digital clock pass the minutes in the dark. That happened to her at home sometimes, on nights she knew she had to get up early the next day. Many times, at Amy's, Katie and Amy would just fall asleep talking. But the conversation wasn't flowing quite as freely with Whitney. *That's okay,* Katie told herself. *It makes sense, actually. We just don't know each other yet. Soon we'll have a lot more to say to each other.*

"Let's play Around the World," Whitney suggested. "I say the name of a place and then you say another place name beginning with the last letter of the place I just said. Like, I say Connecticut, which ends with a T, so you say something that starts with T, like Tanzania. That ends with an A, so I say something that starts with A, like Amazon. Then you say, like, Nairobi. We keep going until someone gets stuck. Or falls asleep."

"Okay, you start," said Katie.

"Belgium," Whitney said immediately.

"Um . . . Montana," Katie said.

"Good!" Whitney said. She seemed impressed that Katie had caught on so quickly. "Antwerp."

"Where's that?" asked Katie.

"Belgium."

"Oh. Okay, um, Pennsylvania."

They continued playing. Whitney was really good at the game, having lived in so many places, but Katie kept getting stuck. She could only think of U.S. state names, or towns in Connecticut, while Whitney was coming up with places like Mongolia, Odessa, and Zaire.

Whitney fell asleep waiting for Katie to think of a place, and Katie lay there and thought about caramel chocolate apples and how much fun that booth was. And how it was good that she was making a new friend. She decided that she was having a pretty good time.

But she also couldn't help thinking about how she could hardly wait till Amy came back for Harvest Fair. She rubbed her fingernails in the dark. The polish felt smooth and cool. She remembered how carefully Amy had applied it.

Katie had thought that Whitney was asleep, but then she heard her humming softly. After a few rounds, she recognized the tune as "Rock-a-Bye Baby." Katie's mom used to sing her that lullaby, and Katie was strangely comforted by Whitney's pretty humming of it. Maybe Whitney knew that she was a little worried about falling asleep? Wow, that was pretty sweet. Finally Katie started to drift off to sleep.

She was in that weird state between being awake and being asleep when she heard something strange. Actually, strange didn't even begin to describe it.

It was her name. Being chanted softly.

Katie, Katie, Katie.

All around her. And then a little bit louder.

It wasn't being chanted in a good way, either, like at

a sporting event, where people would chant their team name happily: *Ti-gers! Ti-gers! Ti-gers!* It was chanted in a slow, quiet way, like a low growl.

Katie, Katie, Katie.

CHAPTER 7

Katie woke up with a jolt. She was no longer in the in-between-waking-and-sleeping state.

The chanting was still happening. *It's no dream . . . it's real!* she thought.

Katie, Katie, Katie.

Where was it coming from?

Katie looked over at Whitney in bed. She was fast asleep on her back and had her arms crossed across her chest. *Such a strange way to sleep,* Katie thought. But she clearly had other things to worry about besides Whitney's sleeping position.

Katie instinctively grabbed her cell phone to use as a flashlight. She turned it on and felt a little better just seeing its familiar soft blue glow. She held it up and tilted it a bit to look around. The dolls were just sitting there like they'd been before, all along the edges of the room, but the light from the cell phone made their faces look even creepier. Their mouths weren't moving, but she was suddenly sure it was the dolls that were chanting her name.

She couldn't say how; she just knew. And she was frozen with fear.

Then the single word *Katie* turned into a full sentence. It was unmistakable.

The sentence was this: *Katie, get out!*

And again. *Katie, get out! Katie, get out!*

A scream froze in Katie's throat, like in a dream. When she finally tried hard and started to scream, she stopped herself. The dolls were making themselves crystal clear. They didn't want her there. Who knew what they would do if she were to scream?

So she lay back down and closed her eyes and did not move a muscle. In other words, she played dead. Like a possum. A terrified possum.

CHAPTER 8

Katie used the same thoughts as before to talk herself down. The chanting had stopped. But she'd started her own chant in her head: *Your imagination runs away with you. You get a little carried away. You had too much sugar today. A figment of your imagination. Never any ghosts or burglars. Your imagination runs away with you. You get a little carried away. You had too much sugar today. A figment of your imagination . . .*

Or, she realized, using all her powers of reasoning, *you were dreaming.* She must have been. It had been a dream. It had just seemed so real, the way dreams do.

When she was younger, her dad had explained to her that dreams come from the subconscious. While you sleep, your brain doesn't just turn off. Things that happened during the day—things you saw, heard, and felt—can find their way into your dream in strange ways. She understood that her mind created all her dreams, and that anything could happen in a dream. And it often seemed real. Sometimes it seemed realer than real: like, superreal.

At the breakfast table, her parents would always ask her, "Did you have any dreams last night?" She'd describe a dream and ask her parents what they thought it meant. They'd never answer. They'd only ask more questions, like, "What do you think it meant?" or "What did it mean to you?" which was kind of annoying because sometimes she had absolutely no idea.

Being a therapist and a psychology professor, her parents sure loved to talk about dreams. Katie decided a little self-therapy was in order. *Okay, what was that all about?* She tried to think very logically. What questions would her parents ask her?

They might say something like, *Tell us more about how you felt about the dolls when you first saw them.*

She answered the pretend question. *I thought they were weird. But it really seemed like Whitney thought they were her friends. I thought it was kind of babyish.*

She lay there for a minute until another thought popped up. *But actually, I wish I had more friends.*

And there she was, having a pretend conversation with her parents:

Dad: You wish you had more friends. You've been lonely since Amy moved.

Katie: Yeah, and Whitney must be lonely too, being the new girl. So she pretends her dolls are her friends. I guess it's not such a bad idea.

Dad: And the dolls were telling you to get out.

Katie: Yes. And it was so real and so creepy!

Mom: So it was like you weren't welcome, even in the house of your new friend.

Katie: Um, that's an understatement. I was totally unwelcome. They said "get out" like they were zombies and wanted to keep me away from Whitney. And she's basically my only friend so far in seventh grade.

Mom: It would be really bad if something

stopped you from making a new friend, wouldn't it?

Katie: Totally.

Dad: It seems like that's what was happening in your dream. If the zombie dolls were telling you to leave, you wouldn't be able to go to Whitney's house again, right? You couldn't make a new friend. You'd stay lonely. Kind of the worst-case scenario.

Katie: Totally.

Mom: You've been really worried that you wouldn't make a new friend after Amy moved. But you've been so brave, trying to make a new friend. It's been a rough week, but you've hung in there. And now, when your guard is down, in your sleep, your anxiety is catching up with you.

Dad: Right, in your dream.

Katie had to admit, she was impressed with this improvised exercise. Maybe she should be a therapist like her mom. She felt so much better!

Okay, she told herself. *It was definitely a dream. Dad is right. Our brains* are *amazing.* She zipped up her sleeping bag a little more, so she would feel more protected as she went to sleep. She felt much better and more relaxed after her little pretend therapy session, but it felt good to control the zipper. Her sleeping bag was like a safe pouch, and if she zipped it up as much as she could, she knew she would sleep better. She actually tried zipping it completely so that no part of her would be exposed, but she thought she might suffocate. So she unzipped it enough to breathe. And finally, she slept a dreamless sleep.

When she opened her eyes, the room was bright. For a minute she couldn't remember where she was. But the first thing her eyes focused on were the dolls, which were actually pretty close to her, since she was sleeping on the floor. They sat motionless and stiff against the wall, exactly as they had when Katie first entered the room. There was Penelope, there was Irene, there was Veronica. She was at Whitney's house, she'd slept over, and she'd had a bad dream, but she was okay.

As she slowly awoke, her dream came back to her in bits and pieces. She remembered the dolls chanting, and she certainly remembered being scared. But it all seemed so silly now, and as she tried to recall the details of the dream, she felt them slipping through her fingers as if she were clutching a handful of sand.

She looked up at Whitney's bed, which was empty. Whitney must already be downstairs. Katie heard what she thought of as "morning kitchen sounds": the refrigerator opening and closing, plates and silverware clinking, water running, cabinets opening and closing, people moving around.

Now that she was older, she was sleeping later, and usually her parents were up before she was. She liked being home and waking up and hearing morning kitchen sounds. She always looked forward to going down to the breakfast table, where she knew something good would be waiting. She had even tasted coffee for the first time this summer, a sip from her mom's mug, but she couldn't believe how bad it tasted. Her parents had laughed and told her it was an acquired taste.

"That's what you say about everything that tastes bad!" Katie had groaned as she rolled her eyes. After that, she decided to stick with her tried-and-true favorite, chocolate soy milk.

Whitney and her dad must be eating breakfast. I wonder where her mom is, Katie thought. *Maybe her parents are divorced.* Most kids Katie knew whose parents were divorced lived with their moms, though. Usually their dads lived nearby. But even so, even if her parents were divorced and Whitney lived with her dad, Whitney didn't talk about her mom. She barely acknowledged her father, either. Was her mother dead? Katie knew a few kids who had lost a parent. It seemed like the worst thing that could ever happen. Katie thought she'd ask Whitney about it, but she couldn't think of a polite way to do it. Just asking, "Where's your mom?" seemed kind of blunt.

Speaking of dads, hers was supposed to come at noon, and it was nine fifteen. She went downstairs, realizing she hadn't even seen the rest of the house. She and Whitney had spent the whole time in Whitney's room. She didn't even know where the kitchen was. But then she heard Whitney and her dad talking, and followed the sounds. She slowed down a little bit, suddenly curious to hear. She knew it was wrong to eavesdrop, but she couldn't help it.

"You always do that," Whitney was saying. "And it

really upsets me. You upset me just like Mommy used to."

What does he always do? Katie wondered.

"I'm sorry, honey," Whitney's dad said softly. "I'll try not to do it anymore."

"You'll *try* not to do it, or you won't do it? They're two very different things."

"I *won't* do it," her dad said, almost like a little kid. *Wow, that was kinda harsh,* Katie thought. She walked into the room as if she hadn't heard a thing. Whitney was fully dressed. She sat at the kitchen table, reading the back of a cereal box and calmly eating a bowl of cereal and milk. Her dad had already left the room.

"Hi," Whitney said loudly, and she smiled widely. In the morning light her light eyes looked piercing. Her skin looked so light in the bright kitchen it was almost see-through, and she sat up straight and stiffly . . . as stiffly as the dolls in her room.

With one big *whoosh*, all the talking down that Katie had done on herself after the "dream" was wiped out. She just *knew* it had not been a dream. It had been real. Those dolls were so creepy . . . and so was Whitney, with her crazy blue eyes and her old-fashioned room and her porcelain skin and her too-loud voice and her nightgown and her long silences and her peeled grapes and the way she spoke to her dad.

"Good morning! There's cereal here for you," Whitney said as if she were working at the front desk at a hotel and Katie was a customer. Whitney was acting too much like everything was fine, as if she were trying to convince Katie of something.

Katie had a gut feeling that she had to *get out*. Just like the dolls had told her. Like, immediately. She didn't say a word. She ran upstairs as if being chased, got dressed as fast as she could, rolled up her sleeping bag, and shoved her pajamas into her backpack. She bolted out of the house without going into the kitchen to say good-bye. Once outside, she ran down the driveway and called her dad from her cell phone, saying to pick her up on the corner of Whitney's street, Alabaster Way, as fast as he could.

She stood close to the street sign so her dad would see her. Alabaster Way. What kind of a street name was that? It sounded like the name of a ghost.

CHAPTER 9

Katie had never been happier to see her dad's car. Or her dad, for that matter.

"Kookaburra!" he said when she got in. "Are you okay? What happened?"

"I really don't know where to start," Katie said, still shaky but feeling better already as the car started moving. She suddenly loved the inside of the car, and she suddenly loved driving with her dad. She could drive with him all day.

"Well, why don't you start at the beginning?" her dad said with a grin. "A very good place to start."

Katie took a deep breath. "When I got there, I noticed all her dolls. She has a million dolls, the old-fashioned kind. And she wanted to play with them, which I thought was weird and babyish. But I went along with it."

"Right," her dad said. "When in Rome, do as the Romans do, right?"

"That's kind of what I thought," Katie said. "And the rest of the time was okay. It was pretty fun. We drew pictures with these cool glitter pens, and her dad brought us food on a tray. We played a word game before we fell asleep. But then I thought I heard the dolls chanting my name."

"Chanting your name?" her dad said. Now she really had his attention. "Out loud?"

"Yes," she said. "And I decided it was a dream. Until they started chanting 'Katie, get out.' I almost peed my pants, I was so scared."

"Wow, honey," her dad said slowly. She could tell he was trying to act all normal and nonjudgmental, but the concern on his face was evident. Suddenly Katie felt sort of silly . . . and more than sort of crazy.

Her dad looked like he, too, was wondering if she'd gone bonkers. "Then what happened?" he asked evenly.

"I tried to figure out if it was a dream," Katie went on. She saw a flash of relief on her dad's face. "I thought about what you and Mom might say about a dream like that and why I had it. Like you do at the breakfast table."

"And what did you think we might say?" her dad asked. Katie repeated the imaginary conversation almost line by line.

Her dad was quiet when she had finished. Then he said, "That was very insightful, Katie." He seemed proud.

"Thanks," Katie said. "It made perfect sense, and I was sure it was a dream. And I fell asleep and I didn't dream anymore. But then this morning . . . I don't know. I just got freaked out all over again when I saw Whitney sitting at the breakfast table. She was sitting all stiff like the dolls. And I just had to get out of there. I just had to."

"You got really spooked, huh?"

"You think?" Katie said sarcastically, but she was smiling.

"Maybe you were right, honey," her dad said. "Maybe it *was* too soon to have a sleepover. Maybe you need more time to adjust to Amy being gone. I'm sorry we pushed you when you were just listening to your gut."

"Yeah." Katie nodded. She felt so much better. "I think that's it."

"Always trust your gut," her dad added. "Don't let anyone stop you."

When they got home, there was an e-mail from Amy.

Hey K,

   Hope you had a good time at your sleepover. Did she have a trundle bed? Ha-ha. Guess what I did yesterday? There is a teen karaoke place here, and Kira, her twin brother, Kyle, and two of their friends (who are also in my classes) were going. On Friday at school, Kira invited me and so I went and it was SO MUCH FUN! You rent a little room and do karaoke, and they bring you soda and snacks. We were in the little room for almost three hours! I even sang, can you believe? And I did a duet with Kira's brother, which was so embarrassing, but I did it on a dare.

   There was a frozen yogurt place next door to karaoke called Swirled World. You choose a combo of yogurt flavors, and they swirl them together. Then you add whatever toppings you want. Here's what I had: blueberry and vanilla yogurt swirled together. Then my toppings were banana, strawberry, and blueberry. (Kira had chocolate-vanilla swirl with gummy bears and Fruity Pebbles topping. Can you believe that? She is really wacky!) I can't believe I am saying this, but I think it might even be better than the candy apple booth at Harvest Fair. And much healthier, too! ☺

Hmmm, what else . . . I am running out of clothes because our stuff still hasn't come, so Kira lent me some of her clothes. We are the exact same size.

Love, A

Karaoke and frozen yogurt, Katie thought. *That kind of beats nightmares of an army of zombie dolls. Guess Amy had a better night than me. Okay. That's okay. She has to make new friends. I wouldn't want her to not make new friends. It doesn't mean we won't always be best friends.*

Though she had to keep repeating that to herself, the same way she had repeated, *It's only a dream* last night.

She wrote back right away.

Hey A, The sleepover was fine until I had crazy dreams. Like, totally crazy. Glad you had so much fun. I wish we had karaoke here. The frozen yogurt sounds good, but how could you say it's better than the caramel apple booth! That is just crrrrrazy! CRA-AY-ZEE! (But not as crazy as my dreams.) ☺

Love, BFF

Amy wrote back a few minutes later.

Oh no! Did you eat cheese before you went to bed? Remember how cheese gives you bad dreams? Cheese dreams! Well, gotta go.

Wow, I did eat cheese on the tuna melt, Katie thought. *It was a very cheesy tuna melt. Cheese dreams! That explains it.* Also, Whitney had told her that Wisconsin, where she had just lived, was a major cheese state. It was actually kind of bizarre how Whitney knew all these details about cheese production in Wisconsin.

"Approximately thirteen thousand dairy farms produce an average of twenty thousand pounds of milk each year, which means a *lot* of quality cheese for Wisconsin!" Whitney had announced proudly.

"How do you memorize these facts?" Katie marveled.

"I'm a cheese head!" Whitney said.

Katie laughed. "I love cheese."

"Me too. Actually, I know a fun game to play about cheese. Wanna?"

"Sure," Katie said. A game about cheese sounded quite wonderful!

"Its called Forever Cheese. You say the three cheeses you would eat if you could eat only three cheeses for the rest of your life."

"That's easy," Katie said confidently. "My favorites are cheddar, American, and swiss."

"Okay, it's your decision, but I'd think more carefully," Whitney advised. "Remember, they're the only cheeses you can eat for the rest of your life. So, what would you have on your pizza and other Italian food?"

"Ohhh." Katie sighed. "I'd really need mozzarella and Parmesan."

"Right!" Whitney nodded vigorously. "You need to cut a cheese from your original list to make room for one or both of those."

"Cut the cheese!" Katie said, and they both cracked up.

"Wanna know mine?" Whitney said. "I figured them out a long time ago. First, Parmesan, because it's a very versatile cheese. You can use it on so many different things and get a lot of flavor. Second, cheddar, because it's also quite versatile and it's from Wisconsin, so I really fell in love with cheddar there. And third, Gouda, because wherever I've lived in Europe there's been amazing Dutch Gouda cheese, and it's a taste like no other. It comes in a big round wheel, and I like to eat it just plain."

"Wow, you've really got your cheese all figured out," Katie said with a laugh. "Okay. I've edited my list. Cheddar, Parmesan, and swiss. I think that covers all my cheese bases. And I hope I never have to really choose. I love cheese too much to limit myself."

"Nice," Whitney said. "I hope you never have to choose either. But I think those three would serve you very well forever."

"Thank you very much. Hey, I just remembered something totally random," Katie said. "My parents told me we should look at the moon tonight. It's going to be a full moon, and a harvest moon. It's supposed to be big and, like, kind of a yellow-orangey color."

"Cool," Whitney said. They went to the window, and there it was as promised: big, low, and yellow-orange. It was an amazing full moon.

Whitney looked at Katie, her eyes wide. "GOUDA MOON!" she exclaimed, and they both cracked up.

So maybe between the eating of the cheese, the talking about cheese, the playing of Whitney's cheese game, and staring at the crazy Gouda moon, the cheese dreams had kicked in.

Katie sat staring at Amy's e-mail on the screen for a few minutes. She knew it was just a fast e-mail, but she couldn't help thinking, *Why didn't Amy sign it BFF? We always sign everything BFF.*

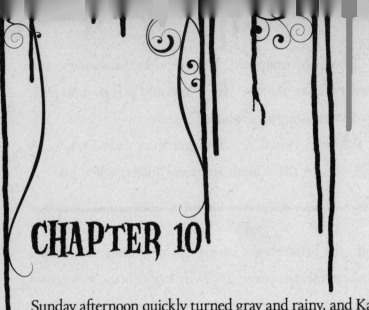

CHAPTER 10

Sunday afternoon quickly turned gray and rainy, and Katie was relieved to have no plans except build-your-own taco bar for dinner with her parents and movie night at home. After lunch, she crawled into bed with Zappers for a nap, which she hardly ever did. But she'd slept pretty badly last night and was happy to be in her own bed in her own room—a room that didn't totally creep her out. She actually slept for a few hours, until her mom came in and sat down on her bed and started massaging her feet, which was the only way to wake her up without her getting cranky.

"You don't want to sleep through the tacos, do you?" her mom asked.

"Definitely not." Katie smiled sleepily. She felt near normal again.

"Good call," her mom said. She was petting Zappers as she looked at Katie. "Hey, Dad told me about what happened at Whitney's. How are you feeling now?"

Katie groaned. "Um, a combination of creeped out and mortified," she said. "I guess about ten percent creeped out and ninety percent mortified."

"What do you think your experience was all about?" her mom asked. It was exactly the kind of question she tended to ask, and it required more than a few words of response. Katie supposed this was how she dealt with her patients.

"I think it was just too soon for a sleepover," Katie said, hoping this would be the end of the conversation. "That's what Dad said."

"Is that what you think?" her mom asked. "That may have been Dad's idea, but did it ring true for you?" Again, a totally typical thing for her mom to say.

"Yeah, it really did," Katie said, rolling onto her back and realizing that it was pretty much the truth. "And you know what else rings true to me?"

"What's that?"

"Build-your-own taco bar."

Her mom laughed. "Get up, then, girl!"

Katie sat up. "But you know what? I'm going to skip the cheese on my taco tonight."

Her mom pretended to be totally stunned. Her mouth hung open. "Skip the cheese? You love cheese!"

"I know. But have you ever heard of cheese dreams? Amy says if you eat cheese before bed, you get weird dreams. Cheese dreams. And I think that was part of my problem last night."

Her mom nodded slowly. "Ahhh, I see. Cheese dreams," she said. "I've never heard of them, but hey, remember the Scrooge character in the Charles Dickens story? He blamed his nighttime visitations on 'a crumb of cheese.' Hmm, I wonder if there's anything to that. I suppose anything's possible when it comes to dreaming."

"Totally," Katie agreed.

"So I suppose this means you'll be having extra olives," her mom said with a wink.

CHAPTER 11

Monday morning came faster than Katie would have liked. She was nervous about facing Whitney, and still embarrassed about how she'd run away. It was too bad Whitney didn't have the kind of phone that Katie could send her a text message on, or an e-mail address. That would've helped smooth things over before they saw each other in school. She was the only person Katie knew who didn't have either. It felt impossible to get in touch, although she knew there was always the good old-fashioned phone.

But there was Whitney in homeroom, smiling brightly when she saw Katie. Her whole face was lit up, and it was if nothing strange had happened and the sleepover had gone as planned, without Katie bolting out of the house like a lunatic, hours earlier than she was supposed to leave, without saying good-bye. Should Katie say something—apologize or something? What on earth could she say? It was all too weird.

Katie wound up avoiding Whitney until lunch, when she could avoid her no more. Whitney sat down and opened her lunch. It was the same as it had been the three days last week: an apple cut into fours, a peanut-butter sandwich cut into fours, four crackers, and four slices of Gouda cheese, each in a separate plastic bag.

"Oh, you forgot your toothbrush! Here," Whitney said, handing it over.

"Thanks," Katie said. "I had another one at home. Hey, what's with the number four?" She pointed to Whitney's food.

Whitney laughed. "Oh. It's my favorite number. Weird, right?" And somehow everything seemed completely normal again. Katie thought it was good that Whitney was acknowledging some of her weirdness. It made her seem not so weird, but who really cared if she was weird? Weird could be fine if a person was nice and interesting enough, and Whitney was both.

It was like Katie's dad always declared when Katie

called something weird: "Normalcy is overrated."

Katie kept checking for text messages between classes. The last e-mail she'd sent Amy, last night before bed, was about plans for Harvest Fair. Katie had drawn up an hour-by-hour schedule for her birthday weekend.

Friday: What time do you arrive? We will pick you up at the airport!

Friday night: Pizza at Sal's, the new pizza place, which you will love!

Saturday morning: Westbrook Diner, just the two of us, for my birthday brunch!

Saturday afternoon: Manicures/ pedicures! Then a walk on the beach if it's not too cold. We can pick shells for you to bring back to California with you.

Saturday night: Birthday cake and Harvest Fair. Or Harvest Fair and birthday cake. Which do you think is better?

Sunday morning: Sleep late—what time do you have to leave? Or can you stay till Monday? I think it's okay to come to school to visit. I bet everyone would love to see you.

Finally, between science and math class, there was a text message.

YO, K——I HAVE TO CHECK WITH MY PARENTS ABOUT THAT WEEKEND.

Katie's stomach lurched. What did that even *mean*? She thought Amy's parents had already promised her she could come. Shouldn't she be buying plane tickets soon?

She wrote back right away, typing as she walked:

OH NO, WHAT DO YOU MEAN, IT'S NOT FOR SURE?

She hit send as she was about to enter the math classroom, not even noticing Whitney walk right by.

"What's the matter? You look terrible," Whitney said.

"Thanks." Katie looked up and smiled sheepishly.

"Sorry, no, I mean . . . you look sad," Whitney explained.

Katie looked at the time on her phone. She had a couple of minutes before class started, so she leaned against the wall and sighed. "I'm okay," she told Whitney. "It's just . . . I was sure Amy was coming back for Harvest Fair and my birthday, and now it doesn't seem so certain. I just got a text from her."

"Oh," said Whitney. She spoke gently. "That's hard. I guess it's a long trip for just a weekend, right? That must be the problem. Because I'm sure she really *wants* to come."

"Whatever," Katie said. Hearing her own anger in her voice, she realized she was equally sad *and* mad. But Whitney was trying to be nice, saying that it was a long trip for a short period of time. And though Whitney had never met her, she seemed to see only the good in Amy, the way Katie used to, before all the doubt and loneliness started creeping in. "I mean, I know. Thanks," she added.

"How's she doing, anyway?" Whitney asked. "Is she doing okay in her new school?"

Katie felt tears spring to her eyes and was slightly horrified. *I've embarrassed myself in front of Whitney enough for one forty-eight-hour period, haven't I?* she thought. But Whitney was looking at her so intently, so kindly.

"She's doing just great," Katie said, her voice breaking

on the word "great." And then Whitney reached over and did something she hadn't done before. She gave Katie a hug. Whitney was kind of thin and tall, and moved slightly awkwardly, as if she hadn't yet grown into her own height. Katie wouldn't have thought a hug from her would feel so warm and cozy. She'd thought it would feel a little stiff. But it didn't.

It actually helped. A little. And as Katie's dad sometimes said, *A little is more than nothing.*

Then the bell rang, and Whitney rushed down the hall. Katie watched her back as she walked quickly away and hoped she hadn't made Whitney late. She blinked back her tears, took a deep breath, and walked into math class. She was strangely relieved to have decimals and fractions to contend with. Sometimes numbers were so easy to deal with, compared to real life.

The next day at lunch, Katie was relieved to see Whitney sitting at their table as usual. It had been a long morning. Rachel and Emma must be officially boy crazy, she had decided. They were nice enough to her, but something had shifted, and they felt very far away. The two seemed closer than ever, which made Katie miss Amy more than she already did.

As soon as they sat down to eat, Whitney said, "So have you heard from Amy?" She seemed to know how important it was to Katie and said it like it was the first item on the agenda.

"No, I have not," Katie said. "Which is weird. Usually she writes back right away."

"Maybe the time difference is messing things up," Whitney said. "That happens to me all the time with my faraway friends in different time zones."

"It's only three hours," Katie said. "And with text and e-mail, it doesn't really matter."

Whitney nodded as if the idea of texting and e-mailing were totally new to her. "You're really upset, aren't you," she said. "I can tell. I don't know you very well, but I can tell."

Katie nodded and looked at her sandwich. She had to admit Whitney had a really nice way about her. She was sympathetic without being too nosy, and, in these moments, spoke with a gentleness that was comforting.

"What's the very worst thing that could happen?" Whitney continued. She sounded a little like Katie's mom or dad. But that was okay. Katie knew she had pretty wonderful parents.

"That she's not my best friend anymore." Katie sighed. "That she has a new best friend. This Kira girl. That I won't have a best friend."

Whitney nodded. "Amy's still your best friend. Moving is just *really* hard," she said. The way she said it, Katie knew she spoke from experience.

"I know," Katie said, nodding slowly. But the truth was, moving didn't seem that hard on Amy. It seemed like she was having a *great* time with her *great* new friends at her *great* healthy yogurt place in *great* California.

"I know this firsthand, better than anyone," Whitney continued. "Amy needs to make some new friends in her new school. She's probably relieved that she met this girl Kira. It doesn't mean that you are being replaced in her heart."

"I know." Katie took a deep breath. The conversation was really making her lose her appetite.

"Plus, a person can have more than one best friend," Whitney continued. "For instance, I think that you're going to be my best friend here. But I have other best friends from all the places I've lived."

That's really sweet, Katie thought to herself. It had never occurred to her that a person could have more than one best friend, but Whitney sounded like she knew what she was talking about.

Katie looked at Whitney and smiled.

CHAPTER 12

The next day after school, Katie got an e-mail from Amy.

> Hey K, How are you? Sorry I didn't write back
> yesterday. Life has been soooo busy (but
> fun). About Harvest Fair, I have to figure out
> about the dates. The thing is, Kira and Kyle
> might be going to a water park that weekend
> with their parents, and they said I should
> come with them. Oh, guess what. Kira says
> Kyle has a "thing" for me, whatever that
> means!

What was she talking about? Kira and Kyle *might* be going to some water park, so Amy suddenly wasn't sure about Harvest Fair? Kyle had a "thing" for Amy? What on earth was a "thing"?

Katie wanted to write back, *Who are you and what have you done with my best friend Amy????* but she stopped herself.

Something else seemed wrong. In her last text message Amy had said she needed to check with her parents. That seemed like a different reason from the one she was giving now. Why was she being so cagey? And thirteen was such an important birthday. They had celebrated Amy's in real style, with the hot-air balloon ride at sunset and then dinner out at a fancy restaurant with her parents. The idea that Amy would blow off Katie's birthday was stunning . . . and heartbreaking.

At school Katie could usually distract herself from thinking about Amy. She loved English class and was constantly surprising herself by really liking math this year. So far, her least favorite class was Spanish.

Spanish was the only class she had with Whitney, and it turned out that Whitney was practically fluent. She was given special projects and could work independently. Sometimes Ms. Marquez would ask her to read aloud, or use her in a conversation demonstration. She seemed to understand everything perfectly. One of her independent projects was to create a teen travel guide to Mexico City. Ms. Marquez explained that everyone would get to read it when it was finished, and that she would post it on some Spanish-language travel sites online.

"I didn't know you spoke Spanish," Katie had said to her at one of their first lunches.

"*¡Sí, hablo Español!*" Whitney had said casually. "*Yo vivía en la ciudad de México por un año.*"

"Um, translation, please."

"Yes, I speak Spanish. I lived in Mexico City for a year."

"Where haven't you lived?" Katie teased, and Whitney laughed.

But it turned out to be great for Katie that Whitney was so good in Spanish, because Katie was struggling a little in that class. She'd gotten an eighty-five on her first quiz, which sent her into a bit of a panic. She didn't usually get below a ninety on anything.

So when it was time for the second quiz, Whitney helped her memorize her vocabulary list over lunch. Whitney would say the word in Spanish, and Katie would say it in English.

"*La guitarra,*" Whitney said, rolling the R beautifully. It sounded like music.

"Easy. Guitar," Katie said.

"*Sí, bueno.* Okay. *Tocar.*"

Katie knew this one. "To play."

"*Excelente. ¿Sabes cómo tocar la guitarra?*"

"Translation, please," Katie said. "Also, that's not on the list. It's just single words."

"I know, but you can put it together, right?" Whitney asked encouragingly.

"Doubtful. Say it again, please," Katie said.

"*¿Sabes cómo tocar la guitarra?*" Whitney said patiently.

Actually, it seemed to kind of make sense. Did she play the guitar? "*No, no tocar la guitarra,*" Katie said slowly.

Whitney clapped. "Very close. You're really putting it together!" she said. It was so fun to be quizzed by Whitney and her pretty Spanish accent.

As Katie took the quiz, she felt like she had a secret weapon, and she got a ninety-nine.

The next day in homeroom, a Friday, everyone was going around the circle, answering Mr. Armstrong's question: What was one success you had in school this week?

"I finally organized my binder," Rachel said.

"Awesome," Mr. Armstrong said. "Organization can be half the battle. Okay, Whitney, you're next."

"I got ahead in science with my independent research on the circulatory system," she said.

"Nice, Whitney," Mr. Armstrong said. "Why do you think you were able to do that?"

"I just like it so much it doesn't seem like work." Whitney shrugged, and Katie noticed Rachel and Emma rolling their eyes at each other.

They're mean, Katie thought. *They're just mean. And now I officially don't care that they've been cold to me this year.*

It was Katie's turn. "I got a ninety-nine on my Spanish quiz," she said.

"¡Qué bueno!" Mr. Armstrong said. What, did everyone speak Spanish now? "And to what do you attribute such success?"

"Whitney speaks Spanish," Katie explained. "And she helped me memorize the vocab list at lunch, before the quiz."

"Thank you, Katie, for helping me introduce my next topic," Mr. Armstrong said. "Okay, guys, here's the deal. I know seventh grade is a big change from sixth, and I'm getting the feeling that most of you are a little stressed out. Is that a safe generalization?"

Everyone nodded yes immediately. The truth was, there was a lot more homework in seventh grade, and you had to organize yourself better. And your grades mattered more. If you were going to go to private high school, which some kids did, then your grades counted. But parents seemed more concerned with grades this year than last, no matter what. It seemed like the beginning of high school or something.

"So you're going to join forces. You're each going to get a partner, and that partner is going to be your resource. If you're at home and you don't understand your math assignment, you can call or e-mail or text your partner. Or if you have a test the next day, you can study together. Every day in homeroom, you'll touch base with your partner to see how things are going."

Hey, it's the same idea as study buddies, thought Katie. *Do all the homeroom teachers in the country get together at conventions and think of things like this?* But then she thought about who her study buddy might be, and she realized she would be pretty psyched if hers were Whitney.

"I don't want to assign partners because you know

yourselves better than I do," Mr. Armstrong said. "So I want you to each write on a sheet of paper who your top three choices are. Number them one, two, and three. Then fold it and hand it to me. I'll look at everyone's choices and determine who should be partners. Ready?"

Everyone started writing on their papers. Katie looked over at Whitney, who was looking directly at her.

Katie wrote, "1. Whitney, 2. Nobody, 3. Nobody." She folded up her paper and gave it to Mr. Armstrong.

Whitney wrote simply, "I only want Katie." She, too, folded her paper and handed it to Mr. Armstrong.

It took Mr. Armstrong a few minutes to read everyone's choices and announce the results, but by the end of the homeroom period, Katie and Whitney were study buddies.

CHAPTER 13

As the weeks approaching Harvest Fair passed, time seemed to speed up. Katie guessed that was good because sometimes Amy wouldn't reply to a text or e-mail for a week. Katie tried hard to not take it personally. She texted:

A, HEY! HOPE YOU ARE HAVING A GOOD WEEK.
DO YOU HEAR A LOT OF SPANISH IN CALIFORNIA?
I BET YOU HEAR MORE THAN I DO. SO FAR IT IS
MY HARDEST SUBJECT. OH GUESS WHAT, I HAVE
A STUDY BUDDY TOO. HER NAME IS WHITNEY.
(SHE'S THE ONE I HAD THE SLEEPOVER WITH.)
DO HOMEROOM TEACHERS GET TOGETHER TO
INVENT THIS STUFF? OH WELL, IT'S GOOD,

ACTUALLY. BUT I MISS YOU SO MUCH. TOO
MUCH.——BFF

Amy responded *four* days later:

HOLA K, CALIFORNIA WEATHER IS THE BEST!

Huh? Amy's response had nothing to do with Katie's
text. It was like she hadn't even read it.

HOLA A, LUCKY! THE LEAVES ARE BEGINNING
TO CHANGE HERE, WHICH IS PRETTY, BUT YOU
KNOW HOW I HATE WINTER. YOU SHOULD'VE
LEFT ALL YOUR SWEATERS HERE FOR ME, YOU
DON'T NEED THEM THERE!——BFF

Another week passed.

I TOTALLY SHOULD'VE LEFT THE SWEATERS. KIRA
AND I SHARE ALL OUR CLOTHES. IT'S SO FUN!
OH, GUESS WHAT, WE GO TO SWIRLED WORLD
SO MUCH WE ARE NOW ON THEIR "FAVORITE

CUSTOMERS" BOARD. OUR PHOTO IS UP ON
THEIR WALL. WE ARE FAMOUS! AND I AM
GETTING SUPERHEALTHY. WE JOG!

Superhealthy? thought Katie. *Amy "double-bacon cheeseburger" Fitzgerald? Jogging? Is she for real?*

The more Katie looked at the text message, the more she was convinced someone had stolen Amy's phone and was writing these messages. *Also, hello, famous for what?* Katie thought sadly. *Ditching your best friend for a new one?* But she tried to understand, and she wanted to keep the conversation going. She wrote right back.

I ALWAYS KNEW YOU WOULD BE FAMOUS. I
CAN'T WAIT TO SEE YOU! DID YOU GET YOUR
TICKETS YET?——BFF

No response. Then, a few days later, there was this:

K, I'M GOING TO HAVE TO COME VISIT ANOTHER
TIME. THAT WEEKEND IS LOOKING BAD FOR ME

BECAUSE OF THE WATER PARK PLANS, KYLE SAID
HE REALLY WANTS ME TO COME. MAYBE IN THE
SPRING?

That weekend is looking bad for you? Katie thought. *The only bad thing about it is that you chose your new friends over me.* She was so upset she couldn't even respond for a few hours. And when she did, she couldn't pretend that everything was okay. She had been pretending long enough.

A, I CAN'T BELIEVE IT. I'M SOOO DISAPPOINTED.
TELL THE TRUTH: AM I NOT YOUR BFF ANYMORE?

And a full three days passed before Amy's response:

K, THAT'S RIDICULOUS!

But it didn't seem ridiculous at all.

In contrast, Whitney always responded right away. As study buddies, they talked on the phone most nights, but Katie had also talked Whitney into getting on e-mail. Whitney seemed anxious, but Katie talked her through it.

"Now you need to think of an address," she said once Whitney was almost set up on the new computer her father had gotten her. "What do you want it to be?"

Whitney was silent.

"It can be anything," Katie said. "Like, mine is kooka123. Kooka's my nickname from my parents. And I had to add the 123 because just plain 'Kooka' was already taken."

"What do you mean, taken?" Whitney asked. *Wow,* Katie thought, *she really is not into technology.*

"Someone else had already chosen it for their e-mail address."

"Oh," Whitney said. Katie waited for her to say something more, but she didn't.

"So, what do you want yours to be?" Katie asked.

Whitney seemed totally stumped. "You think of something," she said. It reminded Katie of when her mom got her grandmother set up online and her grandmother was asking questions like, "What's the difference between online and the Internet?" Her mom had been patient, knowing it was a generational thing.

Katie's grandmother was old, and all this technology was new to her. But it was so funny that Whitney was acting the same way.

Katie tried to channel her mother's patience. "Hmm, well, you have those superblue eyes. How about something like aqua? Hey, how about aquagirl? That sounds cool."

"Aquagirl," Whitney repeated. "I like it. Thanks."

"My pleasure," Katie said, pleased with herself. "Okay, type it in. When you get set up, send me a test e-mail."

"What should it say?"

Katie groaned. "Anything! And welcome to the twenty-first century!" she said with a laugh. "Good-bye!"

About twenty minutes later, she got an e-mail from aquagirl123.

Hello, Katie. This is a test e-mail. I hope you get it. Thank you for helping me.

Katie laughed—Whitney sounded exactly like her grandmother!—and responded:

Hello, your test was successful. You're

welcome for helping you. Now we can be
e-mail buddies.

And Whitney responded less than one minute later.

You know what? This is kind of fun. Oh. I
forgot to tell you. "Aquagirl" was taken, so
I made it aquagirl123 like you. Your friend,
aquagirl123

Katie wrote:

Yay, aquagirl123! Glad to see you finally
online. Tomorrow I'll teach you how to send
attachments. That will help with when we
do homework together. But enough for one
night. You must be exhausted! kooka123

Whitney wrote:

Yes, kooka123, I actually am. Good night! xoxo

Katie smiled, seeing "xoxo." That was sweet. From
then on, Whitney always responded right away to Katie's

e-mails, and they both signed them "xoxo." It wasn't the same as "BFF," of course. Katie didn't think she would want to write that because that was reserved for Amy. But "xoxo" was nice. And when Katie called her, she never got voice mail like she did with Amy. Amy couldn't seem to be bothered to pick up her phone. Like, *ever*.

The week of Harvest Fair, Katie left Amy a voice mail as usual, then pressed the end call button and threw the phone across the couch.

"Whoa!" her dad said, dodging the flying phone. "What's going on?"

"Sorry," Katie said. "Amy never picks up her phone."

Her dad raised his eyebrows. "That must be pretty disappointing," he said.

"It certainly is."

"You've been on the phone and online with Whitney a lot, though, haven't you?" her dad said.

"Yeah," Katie said. "It's nice. It's not the same, but it's nice. She likes to hear from me. It's nice to have someone who's always happy to hear from me."

"Sounds like she's a good friend," her dad replied.

"Yeah . . . she is a good friend," Katie said. And as she said it, she realized she really meant it.

CHAPTER 14

But that little moment of reasonableness and optimism quickly passed. Katie wound up moping around the house so much that week that her parents staged an intervention.

One evening after dinner, Katie sat at the table after her parents had moved into the living room. She was busy picking the polish off her fingers. It had already started chipping, and she couldn't stand looking at it. Each little mini masterpiece now seemed like a big lie. Ladybugs! Watermelon! Rainbows! How simple life had seemed this summer. As she chipped away, she imagined Amy giving a themed manicure to Kira. What was she painting on Kira's nails, *the same exact things?* She thought she might throw up.

Her parents called her into the living room and turned off the television. They patted her spot on the couch, and Katie obediently sat. It seemed serious.

"Kooka, what do you think you can do to make this coming weekend easier on yourself?" her mom said, with her hands wrapped around a mug of peppermint tea.

"Um, make it disappear?" Katie responded sharply. Then she felt bad for being rude. Her parents were just trying to help. It wasn't their fault Amy had decided not to come back for Harvest Fair. Or that she was basically best friends with someone else. Or that she seemed to have a *boyfriend*. Or that she had abandoned Katie on the most important birthday of her whole life so far.

"You've been having a good time with Whitney at school, right?" her dad asked. "And you're on the phone with her every night being study buddies. Maybe you want to invite her over for a sleepover here Friday night. You could bring her to Harvest Fair and then we'd pick you up. You don't want to go to Harvest Fair with your boring old parents, do you?" He grinned.

Katie was still trying to get used to the idea of even going to Harvest Fair at all without Amy, but in her heart she knew she would miss it. She had never not gone to Harvest Fair in her entire life. Actually, some of her earliest memories were of playing in the Pumpkin Patch Playground there. It was a small area set up just for little kids, with haystacks to climb on, piles of leaves and straw to hide in, little toy rakes, and pumpkins of all shapes and sizes. The Pumpkin Patch Playground had seemed like a fall wonderland when she was little, but it looked kind of small and silly to her when she saw it now. But there were so many things she loved: the candy apple booth, the giant slide, and now, this year, maybe even the haunted house.

"Well, what does your gut tell you?" her dad asked.

"Hmm, let me listen," Katie said, looking closely at her belly. They all laughed as she pretended to listen closely.

"Okay, it's saying, 'Sometimes life is lame, but you gotta get yourself to Harvest Fair no matter what, and you should definitely have a sleepover the night before your thirteenth birthday,'" she reported.

Her parents smiled. "Well, there you go. That was a *gutsy* decision!" her dad said, then slapped his leg and laughed. The guy really cracked himself up.

At lunch the next day, Katie and Whitney sat nibbling candy corn that Katie had brought. Whitney had taken exactly four pieces when Katie had offered her some.

"You know how it's my birthday on Saturday?" she asked Whitney.

"Of course I know!" Whitney said.

"Well, I wondered if you wanted to go to Harvest Fair together on Friday and then come to my house for a sleepover," Katie said. She realized with some surprise that she would be very disappointed if Whitney couldn't come. But Whitney's face lit up immediately, and Katie felt a wave of relief that the eve of her thirteenth birthday wouldn't be spent alone.

"I can't wait to go to Harvest Fair. And it's a perfect way to spend your birthday eve," Whitney said. "But I insist that you come to *my* house for the sleepover afterward."

Katie felt that same anxiety she'd felt the first time and replayed the crazy experience she'd had there weeks ago. Even though she'd dismissed it as dreams or her imagination gone wild, she still had a bad feeling in . . . well, in her gut.

"Really? But you've never been to my house," Katie countered, trying desperately to think of a way to decline without hurting Whitney's feelings.

"I know, but I have a special birthday surprise in store for you," Whitney answered.

"Can't you give it to me at my house?" Katie asked, racking her brains for a way to nicely *insist* that Whitney agree to come to her house instead.

But Whitney wasn't budging.

"I can only do it at my house. Sorry," she said.

The two girls looked at each other, and Katie knew she would be the one to give in.

"Okay," Katie relented. "My dad will pick us up at Harvest Fair and drop us off at your house then."

"What's the matter?" Whitney was seeing on Katie's face what Katie was feeling in her gut.

"What? Nothing," Katie lied.

"Come on, I know you," Whitney said. "Tell me what's bothering you!"

Katie immediately felt comforted—Whitney *did* know her pretty well by now. It was so nice having a new friend. It didn't replace Amy, or make that hurt any less, but it made a difference. She took a deep breath.

"Okay, but don't be mad," she began.

"I promise I won't," Whitney said solemnly.

"I got kind of freaked out last time I was at your house," Katie said in a low voice. It felt like a huge weight off her chest to finally tell Whitney this.

"Kind of?" Whitney said. "I'd say 'totally freaked out' is a more precise phrase." But by the way Whitney was smiling, Katie knew she was teasing good-naturedly. "And how did you pack up that fast? You went out in a blur."

Katie felt herself blush. "Um, I was freaked out by the dolls. I had crazy dreams, and the dolls, I don't know, they just spooked me. I guess I just never see that many dolls in one place. It just seems weird. I put all my dolls away last year."

Whitney nodded patiently. She didn't seem mad at all. She seemed happy that Katie was opening up to her. So Katie continued, "Okay, you said you wouldn't get mad, so here's the million-dollar question: What's up with all those dolls?"

Whitney answered Katie's question as if she were a parent answering a curious child's question about, say, what gravity was or why there was traffic on the highway.

"Well, since I've moved around so much, I like to collect one very special doll from everywhere I've lived," Whitney began.

That made sense to Katie. She collected sand from all the different beaches she'd ever been to, put it in little jars with labels, and put them on a shelf in a row. They were like little memories of each place. Sometimes just looking at them put her in a good mood. She'd even alphabetized them.

"And also, my dolls have always been there for me. They're all my very best friends," Whitney added.

Katie got that part for sure. She got it a lot more now than she did before Amy disappeared and blew her off. She wished it was that easy for her to substitute a best friend.

"Right," Katie said. "Okay, I get it. That's cool. Really."

"You're my best friend here, you know that?" Whitney said with a big grin. Katie couldn't help but grin back.

"So you'll sleep over again?"

"Absolutely." Katie nodded for emphasis.

"Oh, goody!" Whitney said. Katie thought it was cute how Whitney had some really old-fashioned expressions. Katie would never say "goody." But when Whitney said it, she really meant it. *Goody.*

"I'll rush home right after school tomorrow to prepare the surprise," Whitney said. "So then you can pick me up and we'll go to the fair. Oh, goody."

CHAPTER 15

Katie sat in the car with her dad and looked at her nails. Her end-of-summer manicure was now gone without a trace. Yesterday she had picked off the last bit—the whitecaps on the waves on her pinkie fingers—after deciding to go to Harvest Fair with Whitney. To look at the whitecaps and think of how Amy was supposed to be there, giving her the birthday manicure, was only making her sadder and madder.

Now she studied her bare fingernails in the late afternoon sun as she and her dad drove to pick up Whitney at her house and go to Harvest Fair.

Whitney was waiting for them on her doorstep, and when she saw their car, she stood up, waved, and jumped up and down.

"Well, she seems happy to see you," Katie's dad said, and smiled over at Katie.

Whitney practically skipped over to the car as it pulled into the driveway. She was wearing an orange hat and scarf with a brown corduroy jacket.

"Hi, Whitney," Katie's dad said as she got into the car and closed the door behind her. "You wore the right colors for the fair, I see."

Whitney had a big smile on her face. "Hi, Mr. Walsh. I figured this was the color scheme for the night."

As they arrived at the fair, Katie's dad said, "Well, you girls are going to have a great time. And Katie is the right person to accompany you to your first Harvest Fair, Whitney. She's a real pro."

"I can't wait," Whitney said.

"You picked a good year to start," Katie's dad told Whitney, stopping the car near the entrance. "It's Katie's first time going to Harvest Fair on her own! Last year we stuck around to chaperone, but this year we know you girls are old enough to handle yourselves at this hoedown." He chuckled, and after the girls had left the car, he waved good-bye.

"Bye, almost-teen daughter!" he called gleefully after

Katie. Katie giggled and pretended she didn't know him.

And soon she and Whitney were at the ticket booth, buying a roll of tickets to use for rides, food, and games, and planning what they would do first. Katie didn't want to be bossy but couldn't help suggesting a schedule. She really did feel like an expert, and she felt responsible for Whitney having a great time at her first Harvest Fair.

"Candy apple booth to get good sugar energy, giant slide, vote for pumpkin carving contest winners, look at the prizewinning apple desserts, go into the haunted house if we dare, play Whack-a-Mole, go on Ferris wheel, go feed the goats and horses, split a fried dough because you've never had one before, watch the fireworks, then get deep-fried Oreos, then call my dad to pick us up. Sound good?" Katie said, counting each activity on a finger, until she ran out of fingers.

"Sounds perfect," Whitney said. "Let's do it."

Whitney respectfully followed Katie's advice at the candy apple booth, creating exactly the same ridiculously sugary confection as Katie: first a thin layer of caramel, then two dips of chocolate, then, while still wet, a dip in a big bowl of M&M's. They laughed as they tried to get their mouths around their enormous creations.

Then they shared a burlap bag on the giant slide and Katie sat in front, like a responsible guide should. They went down it a few times. It was fun to be scared together.

In the contest barn, they had the same opinions about which pumpkin carvings were the best, and voted the same. Then they gazed at the apple pies, apple crumbles, apple crisps, apple cakes, apple streusels, apple turnovers, and apple dumplings, all displayed with their blue ribbons.

When they arrived at the haunted house, though, Katie noticed an anxious look on Whitney's face.

"What's the matter?" she asked Whitney.

"Nothing," Whitney said. So they handed the man two tickets each and went through the metal turnstile that was the entrance to the haunted house.

The first part of the house was a little dark room. Its walls, ceiling, and floors were all painted black. There were little Day-Glo spiderwebs painted on all the surfaces, and some skulls and crossbones. The main thing about the room, though, was that the floor was shifting beneath them, which Katie found more weird than scary. She figured that if the rest of the house was similar, it wouldn't be too scary at all.

Whitney was frozen in place, though, trying to keep her balance. Katie knew the truth. Whitney was scared, just like Katie and Amy had been scared in previous years.

"It's okay, " Katie said gently as they both struggled to keep their footing on the wobbly floor. She could tell Whitney was embarrassed. "Listen to your gut. Do you want to keep going?"

Whitney looked at the moving ground and shook her head quickly.

"Then we shouldn't!" Katie said lightly, and took Whitney's arm. They marched right out of the haunted house the way they came in, not caring that they were going in the wrong direction. Whitney looked paler than usual. Katie began skipping in the direction of the Whack-a-Mole game. "Forget about it. Let's go whack some moles instead. It's very satisfying!"

She could feel Whitney's arm relax and didn't even have to look at her face to know that that its usual color was returning and that she was smiling. Harvest Fair with Whitney was totally fun. Her birthday weekend was going just fine. She understood Whitney's fear, and it felt good to be able to make it disappear. And maybe next year Whitney would be ready for the haunted house.

Katie and Whitney used giant rubber mallets to whack plastic moles into their holes. They each won little pencil-topper prizes. They rode the Ferris wheel and chanted to the operator: "Put us on the top! Put us on the top!" so that he would stop the Ferris wheel when they were at the very top of the ride. And he listened!

From the top, they could see the whole town. "There's our school! There's the firehouse!" Whitney cried, pointing. Katie smiled and nodded like a proud parent. Whitney's enthusiasm reminded Katie of what a great town Westbrook was—something that was easy to forget if you'd lived there your entire life. Sometimes she complained about there not being very much to do, but what other town had a Harvest Fair this good?

Then they went to see the goats and horses, and bought little handfuls of food from a machine to feed them. They held out the food in their open palms as the animals gobbled it up happily. Katie loved the way the goats' furry lips felt on her palm, but Whitney had never done it before and needed a little encouragement.

Soon it was time for "dinner"—fried dough with pizza sauce and Parmesan cheese that you shook on. Katie and Whitney split one because they were full from their crazy caramel apples, and they wanted to leave room for the deep-fried Oreos. They sat at the little picnic table and watched people walk by. Katie knew most people in town, and smiled and said hello to some of her parents' friends.

Just before the first fireworks burst above, Whitney said, "It must be nice to know everyone in your town."

BANG! There was the first silvery, shimmery firework. They both looked up.

"I guess," Katie said. "I've never lived anywhere else."

"I'm jealous," Whitney admitted. BOOM!

"But you live here now too," Katie reassured her. "And you'll meet lots of people, and next year you'll see them here and recognize them."

"No, I won't," Whitney answered sadly. Her voice sounded like it was weighed down with lead. BANG! An orange-and-pink firework dissolved into glittery fairy dust above them.

"Sure you will," said Katie distractedly. The fairy dust fireworks were her favorite. She couldn't take her eyes off it.

"No, I really won't. We're moving again," Whitney said. BOOM!

"What are you talking about?" Katie was sure she was joking.

"For real. My dad got a new job in London." *BANG!*

Katie took her eyes off the sky and looked at Whitney's face and knew Whitney was serious.

"Oh my God, Whitney," Katie said in a voice that didn't sound like hers. She couldn't believe it. How could it be? She was finally starting to feel that Whitney was a real friend . . . maybe even a best friend. And she had just gotten here! How could she be moving again? What was the point of making new friends if they just kept moving? *BOOM!* Red, white, and blue fireworks shimmered down.

"When?" Katie finally asked.

"I don't know. Pretty soon, I think," Whitney said. They sat in silence and watched the rest of the fireworks show. Katie didn't know what to say. Her heart sank to her stomach.

"Let's get the Oreos and then call your dad," Whitney finally said.

CHAPTER 16

Back at Whitney's, there were boxes everywhere. It was just like the last time she had visited. Katie was shocked. They were packing already? Had they even unpacked? How soon were they moving, anyway?

Whitney seemed to read Katie's mind. "My dad doesn't get a lot of notice when he has to change jobs," she said. "But don't worry. I have a plan. We'll always be together."

Katie couldn't imagine what such a plan might be, given that Whitney would be moving to *England*, but she was touched by the sentiment. They started up the stairs to Whitney's room. Once there, Katie rolled out her sleeping bag next to Whitney's bed.

As Katie straightened out her sleeping bag, Whitney

brushed confectioners' sugar off Katie's arm. The fried Oreos had been covered in the stuff, and their faces had been well dusted by the time they had finished those crazy snacks. The Oreos were dipped in a pastry batter, then deep fried, then sprinkled in sugar. When you bit into one, there was a "melted" Oreo inside. It was hard to imagine such a thing, but it was true. It was totally over the top. And the sugar had apparently gotten everywhere.

"Thanks." Katie grinned. "Hi, Penelope," she said to the doll she had chosen as her "friend" during the last sleepover. Whitney seemed so happy that Katie remembered Penelope's name. All the dolls were in the same position as last time, and Whitney picked up one of them to show Katie.

"This one's the mommy doll," she said in a very serious tone.

Katie didn't really get it. Weren't they all supposed to be little girls? But then she noticed that this doll looked a little more adult. Her face was less round than the others, and her hair was styled in a way that reminded Katie of the way her own mom wore her hair, curled up on the ends and kind of puffed up on top.

"Cool," Katie said.

"She doesn't have to work like a lot of moms. She gets to stay home and play with all her friends," Whitney continued. "She helps me throw tea parties."

"Cool," Katie said again. She felt much better about the dolls and wasn't that creeped out by them anymore. She just didn't really have anything to say about the mommy doll.

"Well, I don't know about you, but Harvest Fair wore me out," she told Whitney. "And I'm so sad about you moving. I seriously need to process this news! Can we just go to bed?" She couldn't help but feel really, really bummed out. She just wanted her birthday eve to be over with already. Hopefully things would seem a little brighter tomorrow.

"Yeah, okay," Whitney said. "And I have a new game to play once we turn in."

When Whitney came out of the bathroom, Katie noticed that she was wearing a big T-shirt and boxers, not the nightgown like last time. She was pleased that she had become Whitney's nighttime fashion role model.

"Okay, what's the game?" Katie asked as they lay in the dark.

"It's called Forever Candy," Whitney said excitedly. "It's a little bit like Forever Cheese, but it's different. First we talk about all our favorite candies. Ready?"

"Yup," Katie said. "I'm always ready for that. I love candy."

"Me too," said Whitney. "Okay, my favorites are gumdrops, Butterfinger, atomic fireballs, lemon drops, and black licorice."

"Um, okay, my favorites are—" Katie began.

"Sorry," Whitney interrupted. "I just thought of another. Laffy Taffy. Oh, and Milky Way. And Skittles."

"Are you done?" Katie asked, and they both cracked up.

"I'm done, I promise," Whitney said. "Now you go."

"Okay. Reese's Peanut Butter Cups and Snickers . . . and M&M's . . . and Kit Kats," Katie said.

"Are you done?" Whitney asked, and they cackled with laughter again.

"No," Katie replied. "Not even close. Nestlé Crunch. How could I forget Nestlé Crunch? And . . . um . . . Tootsie Pops. And Nerds. Okay, I'm done."

"Okay," Whitney said. "Now. If you could eat only one of those favorite candies for the rest of your life, what would it be?"

"Are you kidding? What a horrible thing to have to choose!" Katie gasped.

"I know," Whitney said, nodding sympathetically. "That's what makes it a hard game. It's harder than Forever Cheese."

"Okay. Snickers. And M&M's."

"Just one!" Whitney giggled.

"Okay, well, M&M's, I guess," Katie said. "Yeah. M&M's. Ugh . . . that was hard!" She felt truly sad to think about never having those other candies again. Good thing it was only a game.

"Okay, mine is Butterfinger," Whitney said. "But the game was easier for me. I've played it before, so I already had my forever candy picked out."

Katie laughed, but she was already falling asleep. Whitney was softly humming "Rock-a-Bye Baby," like she had on their first sleepover. It sounded so pretty, and Katie actually imagined being a baby being rocked. It was really nice that Whitney hummed her a lullaby. She felt good. It was going to be a good birthday tomorrow. But the good feeling quickly turned bittersweet as she remembered Whitney's terrible announcement about moving. She had forgotten about it during the candy game.

On the other hand, she *was* happy she'd made a new friend. Maybe they would keep in better touch than she and Amy had. Maybe she'd even visit her someday in London. She was glad she had stopped being paranoid and creeped out by the doll stuff. She was really going to miss Whitney and wished that her promise to be together forever could be true, but she knew it couldn't.

She was almost asleep when she heard it.

Her name. Being chanted. Again.

Katie, Katie, Katie.

She squeezed her eyes tight and burrowed down in her sleeping bag. But the chanting only got louder. *Katie, Katie, Katie.*

No sleeping bag in the world could have protected her from what was about to happen.

Then she heard Whitney get out of bed.

CHAPTER 17

Katie had to force herself to open her eyes. She could barely see, but her eyes adjusted to the dark. The night-light wasn't on tonight, unfortunately.

Whitney was sitting directly in front of several of the dolls, in that cross-legged "crisscross applesauce" position she'd used when they first sat down and played with dolls together. Her hands were on her hips, and she was leaning forward, as if having a private conversation with them. She looked like a parent or teacher scolding a child in public, trying not to cause a scene or humiliate the child, but very angry and frustrated nonetheless.

And still Katie heard: *Katie, Katie, Katie.* She plugged her ears with her index fingers—the index fingers that had once featured pretty little ladybugs. One of those ladybugs was the one she'd chipped on her locker, when Whitney had first talked to her. It felt like forever ago.

But the crazy thing was, it didn't matter that her ears were plugged. She could still hear the chanting perfectly. She unplugged her ears. Whitney was whispering harshly over the chanting. "Don't I always treat you well?" She seemed to be directing her anger toward three dolls, ones that were sitting together in a row.

And still: *Katie, Katie, Katie.*

"You know you're my best friends," Whitney continued in her angry hiss. Katie had never heard a voice so quiet and so furious at the same time. When her parents were mad, they tended to raise their voices, not get quieter. She figured Whitney must not have wanted to wake her.

"Now we'll have a *new* friend. Stop this. Just stop it. Don't you *want* a new friend?"

Katie, Katie, Katie. But the chanting was getting softer and softer, until it stopped altogether.

Katie lay perfectly still so Whitney wouldn't know she was awake. Instinctively, she curled up her hands and rubbed her fingernails against her thumbs to stroke her fingertips. She was used to doing that to feel Amy's manicures, feeling the glossy polish and remembering the happiness she'd felt when it was applied. In the terror of the moment, she'd forgotten that the memories of the manicures no longer brought her any comfort. But it didn't matter that she had already picked the manicure off, because she couldn't feel her fingertips. Or her whole hands, actually.

Okay, she thought. *Now I know for sure it's a dream!* She'd never been unable to feel both her hands. Sometimes one arm fell asleep, but not both at the same time. Also, she could still hear the chanting even when she was plugging her ears. That is something that would only happen in a dream.

Yay, she thought. *I'm dreaming.* She was actually kind of pleased. She knew that what she was having was a lucid dream. Her parents had explained that in a lucid dream, the dreamer knows he or she is dreaming. Katie remembered the conversation clearly. She had come downstairs in the morning, just a few months ago, and her parents were having coffee, already having finished breakfast.

"I was reassuring myself that it was only a dream," her mom was saying. "And I was so relieved. I would be so upset if giant butterflies really ate our beautiful rosebush!" Her parents both laughed.

"What on earth are you guys talking about?" Katie had said, yawning and sitting down.

"Your mom dreamed that evil monster butterflies were eating our garden," her dad explained. "But your mom is a lucid dreamer. In her dreams, she often knows she's dreaming. So even in a nightmare, she can reassure herself it's only a dream."

Katie poured cereal into her bowl. She thought for a minute. "That's pretty cool," she admitted. "So you can never really have actual nightmares."

"Right, kind of," her mom said. "Though my dreams aren't *always* lucid. But I like it when they are. It's like being in the audience in a really imaginative movie. Or a really scary movie, depending."

"I don't think I've ever had a lucid dream," Katie said.

"You might sometime," her dad said.

Well, it seemed that her night of lucid dreaming had arrived. Because now Katie couldn't feel her feet, either. *It's only a dream,* Katie thought. *Because I can't feel my hands or feet.*

"Our minds are amazing," her mom would explain

when Katie had bad dreams. "They can make up things that seem realer than real."

"You say that like it's a good thing!" Katie would say, and roll her eyes. But in this case it totally made her feel better. *Even if I have this crazy dream all night, it's okay because it will all disappear in the morning,* she thought. *I probably won't even remember it.*

CHAPTER 18

Sunlight flooded the room and woke Katie up, eyeballs first. As she opened her eyes, she noticed they felt really strange, like her eyelashes were coated in dried glue.

She went to rub the weird feeling from her eyes, but her arm wasn't moving. It was the strangest thing. Just like last night, she couldn't feel her hands or her feet.

Actually, she couldn't feel her arms, either. Or her legs. Katie couldn't feel any part of her body.

She couldn't move at all. It was like when your arm or leg falls asleep and you have that weird dead-weight feeling on your body. But this time it was her entire body that was dead weight.

Okay, she thought. *This dream has gone on long enough. Seriously. I need to wake up NOW!*

The only thing she could feel was her eyes, which she now used to look around. The only parts of her body that seemed to work were her eyes and her brain.

"Your brain is the boss of your body," her kindergarten teacher had explained to the class when they were learning about the five senses. They learned about how you can make your brain tell your body what to do, like jump or sit down. Then your brain tells your muscles to do those things.

But if her brain was the boss of her body, it had just been fired from its job. Because no matter what Katie wanted to do—move an arm, wiggle her toes, stand up and run away—her body was not cooperating. It was like her brain was a telephone that had dialed a phone number, and there was just no answer on the other end. Nothing was working.

She saw that she was sitting among the dolls, right next to Penelope, the doll in the sailor suit that Whitney had told her was Dutch. Penelope was staring straight ahead with her crazy light-blue eyes and stiff plastic eyelashes.

Then Katie used her eyes to look down at her body. And what she saw made absolutely no sense to her or to her brain or to anything. She was sitting in exactly the same position as Penelope, with little arms at her side, her back against the wall, and little legs sticking out.

Katie was miniature!

Whitney sat "crisscross applesauce" a few dolls away, holding a red lollipop to Irene's mouth.

"Oh, Irene, I know," she said soothingly, as if Irene was a two-year-old about to have a full-blown tantrum. "You hate to go into the boxes. But look. Here's your lollipop!" She touched the lollipop to Irene's porcelain mouth.

"Soon we'll be in a new home, and you'll like it even more than this one, I promise." Then she picked up Irene, put her in a small plastic doll box, closed the lid, and put it in a giant cardboard box full of Styrofoam peanuts.

Whitney moved to the next doll, Veronica. Leaning over in the same comforting yet authoritative way, she held a lemon drop to Veronica's doll lips. "Here's your special treat, Veronica," she said in a singsongy voice, pretending to let Veronica eat the sugared yellow hard candy.

Then Whitney picked up Veronica, put her in a clear plastic box, closed the lid, and added it to the big cardboard box.

She continued on to Penelope. "Who loves her licorice?"

Whitney cooed as she held Penelope close. She held up a black licorice stick to Penelope's mouth. "All sailors love licorice, right? We're going back across the Atlantic Ocean, Penelope!" she said excitedly. "Not too far from where your ancestors came from. Remember when I told you all about Amsterdam?" Whitney put her in another plastic doll box, closed the lid, and added it to the big cardboard box.

Then Whitney's face filled Katie's entire field of vision. It was huge.

Whitney's hand came into the edge of the picture, and so did the thing it was holding: a blue M&M, headed straight for Katie's mouth.

Katie tried to scream, but her mouth wouldn't move.

"Katie! You look so pretty!" Whitney exclaimed. She sounded like a mom backstage at a children's beauty pageant. "Oh my gosh. I knew you'd be such a pretty doll. Look! *It's your forever candy.* See, I got you exactly what you wanted."

Katie wanted to close her eyes and reassure herself that she was dreaming, but she couldn't blink. Her eyes were stuck open.

"I know it was hard to choose, but now you have a lifetime supply," Whitney continued as she tapped the

M&M on Katie's lips, which she couldn't feel at all.

"Oh no, Katie! You didn't tell me you didn't like blue M&M's!" Whitney exclaimed with real panic in her voice. "I guess it wasn't part of the game to get that specific. Oh, wait, no problem. I have them in every color. Here, do you like yellow?" Again she tapped an M&M onto Katie's lips.

Katie tried to signal with her eyes: *What have you done to me, you crazy monster? You insane lunatic!*

Finally Whitney put the M&M on the floor and picked Katie up. As she moved through the air, Katie felt like she was on a horrible ride at an amusement park. Except that this was the total opposite of amusing.

"See, I told you, Katie!" Whitney crowed. "We are going to be best friends forever! Together forever!"

Whitney reached for a small clear plastic doll box like the ones she had put the other dolls in. "And look at how many other best friends you have now. So silly to worry about Amy when you have so many other BFFs, right?"

Then Whitney put Katie in the clear box and closed the lid.

EPILOGUE

The door opened, and Whitney walked into the room with a girl clutching an overnight bag. "This is my room, Shelly," Whitney said, proudly indicating the space with a wave of her arm.

Katie watched from her position across the room. Exactly two weeks earlier, she had been in the black pit of the box, where Whitney had placed her that day on Alabaster Way, when she heard a sharp tearing sound.

"Oh, my Best Friends Forever!" she heard Whitney shriek. "I've missed you all so much. And here you finally are! Who's ready for teatime in London?" Even though Whitney's voice was muffled, Katie thought she sounded happier than ever before.

Some smudgy light had filtered through the darkness. It hurt Katie's eyes, having been in the pitch dark so long. She felt her box shift slightly from side to side. It must have been Whitney brushing away the Styrofoam peanuts. Then she felt some movement from above, which she figured was Whitney removing dolls from the box. More light came in as more dolls were removed, more movement.

From within her box, Katie listened as Whitney methodically unpacked the dolls. She would open each box and cheerfully greet the doll by name.

"Irene! How was your trip? Here's your lollipop. Oh, Veronica, I missed you so much! You were very well behaved on the trip, weren't you? I can tell," she chattered away.

"Here's your lemon drop," she told Veronica. "And here's Penelope! Oh, Penelope. That trip must have been easy on you, being a sailor girl and all. Here's your licorice. And here's Rosa! *¡Hola!*"

Finally it was Katie's turn. Her box was plucked from its Styrofoam nest, and she suddenly saw Whitney's gigantic face before her.

"Katie, I missed you the most," Whitney said in a conspiratorial whisper. "You've never been overseas, have you? Well, welcome to the other side of the pond! This is where the first New Englanders came from! Now you're an Old Englander!" She laughed at her own little joke.

Katie had tried desperately to express herself—her terror, horror, rage, and trauma. But with only eyeballs to work with, she failed miserably. You need eyelids, at the very least, to signal any facial expression, but everything remained frozen.

"Are you hungry? Here's your M&M," Whitney went on as she removed Katie from her small box and again placed an M&M—this time an orange one—to Katie's useless lips. She adjusted Katie's arms and legs so she was in a sitting position, and placed her right next to Penelope. Katie saw that the dolls were arranged along the perimeter of the room, in the same formation as in Westbrook.

Penelope, the "friend" Katie had chosen as the doll to play with at the first sleepover, was now fated to be her neighbor. *Forever*, it seemed.

Katie moved her eyeballs to glance around. There was Whitney's bed, there was the unicorn painting. She could see out the window a little bit, though it was raining outside.

Whitney was still unpacking. "Mommy!" she squealed.

What did she mean, "Mommy"? Katie wondered. Did Whitney's mom live in London?

Maybe she can help me escape from her crazy daughter, Katie thought wildly.

Then Katie realized that Whitney must be talking to the "mommy" doll she had pointed out at their final sleepover. "Welcome to London, Mommy! We'll have so many good tea parties here, but you have to help me serve tea and cookies like you used to, okay? *That's* your job now, remember? Not that stupid office job that kept you away from home so much!"

Whitney paused to adjust the mommy doll's clothing. "What's that?" she asked the doll, leaning in as if to hear her better. "Oh, of course. Daddy's downstairs unpacking. What? You'd like to join us for dinner? That's fine. I'm sure Daddy would like that."

Then Whitney had turned and addressed all the dolls. "Oh, Best Friends Forever, I know it's been a long trip, and I know you must be tired of moving. But listen up. Have you all noticed that we have a new friend? It's Katie! You all remember Katie, right? She's a wonderful friend, and before we met, she thought a person could have only one best friend. Well, we're all going to show her that's not true, aren't we? And you know what else? I'm going to see to it that we have another friend very soon. A British friend. I bet she'll like to have tea parties. Wouldn't it be nice to have a friend who knows how to have a proper tea party?" She gave the mommy doll an apologetic smile. "Not that Mommy hasn't been doing her best . . . but there's always room for improvement, right?"

She leaned close to Katie. "What, Katie?" she asked as if Katie had actually said something. As if Katie could actually speak. "That's right, we're in our new apartment. But remember, they don't say apartment here, they say 'flat.' And instead of bathroom, they say 'loo'! It's quite a lot to get used to, but we'll all manage. We always do."

"What a lot of dolls you have," Shelly said now, looking down along the perimeter of the room.

Whitney nodded, pleased. "Thanks. They're all my best friends. Forever."

"I see," said Shelly. *Rather primly,* Katie thought.

"Well, it's teatime here, right?" Whitney asked Shelly.

"I suppose so," Shelly said.

"Well, let's get started, shall we?" Whitney gestured to the dolls as Shelly stared at her blankly.

"Find a friend," Whitney said. She grabbed the mommy doll and sat cross-legged on the floor.

"Crisscross applesauce!" she said to Shelly. "Once you find a friend, sit crisscross applesauce."

Shelly hesitated. Katie knew what she was thinking: The doll thing was weird, and Whitney was weird too. *Run, Shelly,* Katie thought. *Get out of here!*

Would Shelly be able to hear Katie's thoughts? Katie now realized that when she was hearing the dolls chant, *Katie, get out,* they hadn't been moving their lips. They had been communicating telepathically. That was why she could still hear them even when she plugged her ears. Everything made sense now . . . horrible, horrible sense.

But Shelly simply smiled, reached right for Katie, and obediently sat crisscross applesauce.

"That's Katie," Whitney said. "She's from Connecticut."

"Where's that?" Shelly asked politely.

"It's a state in the northeastern United States, where

I just moved from," Whitney explained. "Katie loves M&M's. They're very popular candies there."

Shelly held Katie on her lap and admired her. Katie knew just how she felt. She must have been trying to think of something polite to say.

"She's lovely," said Shelly. And then she looked at Katie's eyes.

Katie used all her concentration to stare right back.

Run, Shelly! she thought over and over again.

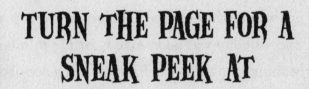

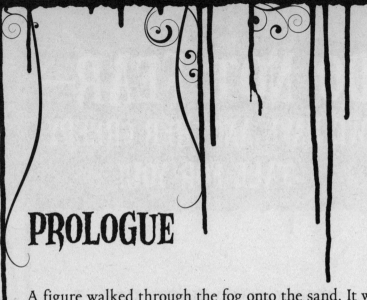

PROLOGUE

A figure walked through the fog onto the sand. It was dark and visibility was poor, except for the thin beam of light shining on the ocean from the full moon above.

He crossed the beach, his fine leather shoes covered in sand up to the silver buckles, but he paid that no mind.

The man wore a thick woolen cloak. He stood in the dark in front of the roaring waves and spoke softly.

"I am sorry for all the days I spent at sea, My Lady. I am sorry for every day that I did not spend with you."

His voice grew louder and he dug his hand into the pocket of his waistcoat to clutch the ring.

"I have burned all your things, My Lady, having kept only this ring to remember you by. This ring that

I slipped on your finger because I loved you so. But you were never the same after that."

He paused, now overtaken by sobs.

Please believe me, he thought.

After a moment, he gathered himself and held the ring above his head.

"This ring . . . this ring is to blame . . . I curse this ring!"

He hurled it into the sea.

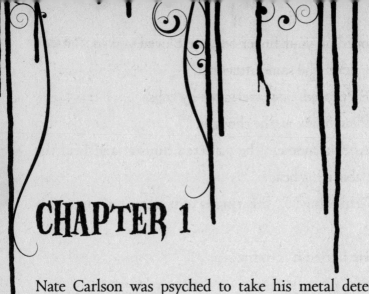

CHAPTER 1

Nate Carlson was psyched to take his metal detector to the beach. The walk to the beach was a short one, because the beach was right behind his house. "The beach is my backyard!" Nate used to tell his friends when he was little. He supposed he got that line from his parents, who said it all the time. It was true, anyway, and pretty awesome. There was a small lawn between his house and the beach, but that was it. Nate felt that wonderful familiar feeling of anticipation as he approached the sand. It was a cloudy, windy day, so he had the beach to himself.

Slipping off his shoes, Nate stepped onto the cool sand. He switched on the metal detector and started walking, scanning the sand back and forth.

A large black bird swooped near his head. As he

ducked, he thought of his twin sister, Lissa. That bird would have sent her running home. Birds totally creeped her out, especially when they flapped too close to her head. He looked up to see a few of them circling above. The others were dive-bombing the water, catching food. They would drop straight down out of the sky, beak forward, disappear into the water, then come up with a crab wiggling in their beaks. It was cool to watch. He had never noticed this type of bird before, but then again he never paid much attention to birds.

BEEP BEEP BEEP! Nate's thoughts about birds were interrupted by the sound of the metal detector going off. Nate bent down and dug around a little. All he found was an old, smooshed-up tin can. He left it there and kept walking, looking at the variety of shells along the tide line. His favorite were the jack-knife clams, which were long and thin, and the jingle shells, which his mother called "angels' toenails" because of their golden shiny hue. Nate's mom said a lot of things that, in Nate's opinion, were pretty corny.

BEEP BEEP BEEP! He dropped to his knees and dug around, not finding anything at all. But when he scanned the spot again, the detector kept beeping. He dug deeper—still nothing. But when he scanned the spot again, *BEEP BEEP BEEP.*

He dug deeper than he ever had before, the sand growing colder and damper the deeper he went. He felt around in the sand for something, anything, but couldn't find the source of what was setting off the detector. But still . . . *BEEP BEEP BEEP.*

He had dug maybe three feet with his bare hands when a tiny flash of gold caught his eye. He fished around until his fingers closed around something. Pulling his hand free, Nate looked in his palm and saw it: A small, perfect ruby ring. *This may actually be treasure,* Nate thought. He sat and stared at it as he brushed the sand off with the bottom of his shirt, squinting to get a better look. Nate realized that the late afternoon sun had gone down, and sky had suddenly grown quite dark. A strange feeling settled over Nate just then. He looked around—did anyone see him find this ring? Should he show someone? The strange feeling grew deeper, and on some level, Nate realized he felt very nervous all of a sudden.

WANT MORE CREEPINESS?

Then you're in luck because P. J. Night has
some more scares for you and your friends!

FOREVER CANDY

In the story, Whitney asks Katie to choose her favorite
candy to be her "forever candy" . . . the only candy she
can ever have again for the rest of her life. Choose your
forever favorites for the following things:

FOREVER BOOK:

FOREVER MOVIE:

FOREVER TELEVISION SHOW:

FOREVER BEVERAGE:

FOREVER FOOD (OTHER THAN CANDY!):

AND OF COURSE . . .

FOREVER CANDY:

YOU'RE INVITED TO ...
CREATE YOUR OWN SCARY STORY!

Do you want to turn your sleepover into a creepover? Telling a spooky story is a great way to set the mood. P. J. Night has written a few sentences to get you started. Fill in the rest of the story and have fun scaring your friends.

You can also collaborate with your friends on this story by taking turns. Have everyone at your sleepover sit in a circle. Pick one person to start. She will add a sentence or two to the story, cover what she wrote with a piece of paper leaving only the last word or phrase visible, and then pass the story to the next girl. Once everyone has taken a turn, read the scary story you created together aloud!

It was late in the evening, well past midnight. My friends slept quietly in sleeping bags all around me, but I couldn't fall asleep. The loud scratching noise coming from the closet was simply too distracting. Didn't my friends hear it too?

Finally I could no longer take it, so I quietly unzipped my sleeping bag and made my way to the closet. The closer I got, the more insistent the scratching became. What was on the other side? I took a deep breath, grabbed the doorknob, opened the door, and found . . .

_____

_____

_____

_____

_____

_____

_____

_____

_____

_____

_____

_____

THE END

A lifelong night owl, **P. J. NIGHT** often works furiously into the wee hours of the morning, writing down spooky tales and dreaming up new stories of the supernatural and otherworldly. Although P. J.'s whereabouts are unknown at this time, we suspect the author lives in a drafty, old mansion where the floorboards creak when no one is there and the flickering candlelight creates shadows that creep along the walls. We truly wish we could tell you more, but we've been sworn to keep P. J.'s identity a secret . . . and it's a secret we will take to our graves!

What's better than reading a really spooky story?

Writing your own!

You just read a great book. It gave you ideas, didn't it? Ideas for your next story: characters...plot...setting... You can't wait to grab a notebook and a pen and start writing it all down.

It happens a lot. *Ideas just pop into your head.* In between classes entire story lines take shape in your imagination. And when you start writing, the words flow, and you end up with notebooks crammed with your creativity.

It's okay, you aren't alone. Come to **KidPub**, the web's largest gathering of kids just like you. Share your stories with thousands of people from all over the world. Meet new friends and see what they're writing. Test your skills in one of our writing contests. See what other kids think about your stories.

And above all, *come to write!*

www.KidPub.com